A Tale Of Karma

...And Forgiveness

D1319144

WHEN GOD CALLED A BOY HOME

WHEN GOD CALLED A BOY HOME

By Paul Hamilton Magid

Library of Congress-In-Publication Data

Magid, Paul Hamilton

When God Called A Boy Home: a profound spiritual journey of healing and forgiveness:

A novel / Paul Hamilton Magid – Manalapan, NJ:

Paul Hamilton Magid, ©2021

p: cm.

ISBN: 978-0-578-85789-3 (print)

1. Spiritual – Fiction. 2. Karma – Fiction. 3. Philosophy, Asian – Fiction. 4. Spiritual Healing – Fiction. 5. Forgiveness – Fiction. 6. Montana – Fiction. 7. India – Fiction.

www.paulhamiltonmagid.com

Author photograph by Sharon J. McQueen

Cover Design by Paul Hamilton Magid

From The Author

We all suffer in this lifetime but we are not here to suffer. We are here to learn and to be loved. This novel exists only because of the amazing love given to me by family and dear friends alike.

Prologue

A young man is walking down a path
Heading in earnest toward the Light
His back is thick
His arms strong
He comes upon an elderly man
Nearly feeble and limping
He stops
And scoops the man in his arms
"Why," asks the old man,
"Are you stopping to carry me?
It will take you longer to reach the Light."
"Why," replies the young man,
"Have I been given this body so strong?
If I return empty handed,
I will only be sent back for you."
The old man nods his weary head
Before resting it on the young man's chest
"That is why you return Home so young.
And I, an old man."

CHAPTER 1

Joseph stood in the shower. Exhausted. Deep in his bones. Still just a boy of seventeen he never imagined he could be so tired. He labored for a calming breath as the cascading water washed the blood from his athletic body.

If only the adversaries who visited upon his nightmares were merely the projections of his own tormented soul. For then he would not have been so shattered. But these same visitors also swarmed him in visions that did not respect the hour of the day.

Animated as they were by a ferocity lacking in mercy, by his reckoning.

Joseph was cursed, or so he believed. He had been under attack for so many of his years on this earth that he had no more tears to give and was crumbling from within. He wondered if time were running out, as no matter how much he labored the burden grew in weight. More so of late and that fact terrified him.

He lifted his face toward the shower head, cupped his hands, and vigorously rubbed his face to make sure the last flakes of dried blood were removed from his nostrils, washing away any remaining evidence of the bloody nose he had given himself while sleeping yet fighting.

To make certain that his mother would never again see such a sight.

Joseph knew that he caused her great pain and she was too kind and loving for another incident of such carelessness on his part. He could have stood there for hours as the steam enveloped him. Staring off in the distance. Perhaps such would be enough time to allow his strength to return.

But he had already overslept many hours and the day would wait no more.

His mother stood over the kitchen sink and washed dishes that were already clean. Her coping mechanism for stress. Bonnie Connell had met her husband John while both were still in high school and neither had ever dated anyone else, knowing as they did that there was no need. Mr. Connell was fourth generation Montanan. Their older son, Billy, at age nineteen completed this family of four. He was hardy in body but soft of nature in the best way possible. Possessed as he was of a gentle way about him, he most took after his mother. Particularly in a desire to look after the youngest member of the family.

It was the boys' great-great-grandfather, widower Tobias Connell, who had settled this southeastern corner of Montana with his sole surviving son round about a hundred years ago in the middle of the 19th century. After some misfortune back home across the ocean.

The details of which were always murky.

Under the Homestead Act as the young country expanded west, most settlers came to focus their energies on farming the one hundred and sixty acres granted to them for free by the government. But Tobias was a good deal more enterprising than plowing land with a single beast of burden for a hardscrabble life. He domesticated wild horses for sale to the U.S. Cavalry and raised cattle which were in high demand, ever more so with each passing year after The Civil War had ended.

The Connell lineage was full of natural businessmen and by the time John Connell's grandfather was at the reins of the family enterprise it wasn't long before he grew their holdings to the twenty thousand acre ranch it was now. For when the plentiful rains of twenty straight years had decided they had visited enough by 1930, most every homesteader abandoned the dry and cracked farmland to head back East in search of work.

Which left each parcel of land to be picked up for mere pennies. Until the twenty thousand acre Connell ranch came together as if by Divine design. Or at least favorable circumstance, for truly the land was awe inspiring to witness.

It was populated by Ponderosa pine trees too plentiful to count. A hundred million would be too low a number, probably two hundred million. Ponderosa was a slow growing and patient tree well suited to this rolling landscape. For the sandstone rock of these foothill mountains was easily eroded by time and the elements. Thus allowing a Ponderosa seed to ever so slightly force the rock to separate and make way for its presence. It matured to have a thick bark and green needles that grew out half a foot in length from the branches.

Each tree was a perfect expression of its immediate environment. For when tightly packed and plentiful, Ponderosa trees competed for earth and sunlight so that each one grew tall and relatively thin and hundreds of feet in towering height. Hoping to outgrow the others. But when a single tree found itself without competition on a stretch of prairie grassland, it grew wide and fat and happy at barely fifty feet high.

Ponderosa was a compliant tree with a soft wood relative to other species. So it was easily chopped and cut or milled into whatever purpose a person might need it to serve. Be that a log cabin, endless miles of fence, firewood, or nearby coal mine shaft support beams.

For comfort Bonnie Connell looked out her kitchen window. While most of their land was untamed foothill mountains chock full of trees, shrubs, brush, and bramble all jostling for real estate amidst the wild underbrush, not so outside her home.

Cresting valleys soothing to behold were just outside her home. With two foot high rich grasslands that swayed in the breeze as if put there for its beauty. To be sure, it had been the swinging farm blades of settlers and family members of days gone by who had cleared the valley that Mrs. Connell looked out upon.

But it was as if Mother Nature had given her blessing to make this place their home. These hundred acres of cleared grassland that rose and fell as it stretched and cradled the Connell family in serenity. Most, anyway.

Their log cabin was built by Mr. Connell upon a friendly plateau of rare flat land that faced due west. Perfect for taking in sunsets over the hills. The back of the Connell house was protected by a foothill mountain that rose up and stood guard behind it. As little boys Joseph and Billy had climbed the three hundred foot of the slope more than a thousand times. More than two thousand even. For the top of it, about as flat as any on the Connell ranch save where their house was built, was a wondrous place. Near it felt to the heavens. A place for boys to laugh and wrestle as they were naturally given to do. Especially brothers.

The house was kept warm in winter by a wood burning stove that warmed rooms in direct proportion to how close they were to it. The kitchen had a refrigerator and a small ice box but most food was stored year round in the root cellar as it had been by Montanans for a hundred years prior, before electricity had made its way to the territory. Such a cellar was nothing more fancy than a hole in the ground dug by a shovel and a sturdy back. It sat adjacent to the house reinforced by wooden planks for the floor, walls, and ceiling with an access door. It was seven feet deep which allowed an adult to stand in it comfortably.

All food stored there was kept by nature year round at a consistent fifty-five degrees, regardless of what cold air swirled above in the harshest winter or hot humid air that sweltered in the heat of summer. Canned fruit and vegetables kept as long as needed in the root cellar, as did the treats of canned jellies, syrups, apple butter and applesauce, which Mrs. Connell made from the fruit she picked from her orchard. Meals were a delight of simple recipes and one helping was never enough. Homemade bread was eaten in abundance.

Neighbors near and far wondered why Mr. Connell had built the house as a single story dwelling with no stairs or second floor. For clearly that made the house half the size it could have otherwise been with more space to spread out bedrooms upstairs.

Mr. Connell always replied that he preferred the open space of a cathedral ceiling and high roof line that a one story house provided. But the truth was that he just knew that his house was not meant to have any stairs.

The gravel driveway was a semicircle that came up from the same paths that sprawled from the red horse barn and wooden fence corrals down below and just enough kissed the wraparound front porch. Said porch was also flat to the earth with no stairs to climb.

The excessive length of the circular driveway was by any estimation inefficient. For rather than be steep in slope and thus the shortest distance on either side leading to and from the house, it meandered. Which while on the one hand had the effect of making for distance further to travel, it also had the undeniable benefit of being a good deal easier for anyone to travel up and down. However a person might need to navigate the terrain. The same rare inefficiency was the defining feature of all the gravel pathways that led all around the Connell ranch.

Such two were the only exceptions to how Mr. Connell lived his life and taught his boys to live theirs. In every element of life, he instilled in them, use as few steps as possible to complete a task. Partly for safety reasons as fewer things could go wrong. And partly because nature did not reward the needless expenditure of energy. So whether opening and closing a fence for cows to travel from one enclosed grassland to another or feeding the horses or digging a well shaft into the side of a sloping hill: use as few as steps as necessary.

Included in that principle was another that warranted its own expression in two parts: put things back where you found them and if they weren't where they belonged, take the time to put them where they should be. Life was more simple and more safe that way. Which in spirit came back around to living life in a way where less things might go wrong.

Mr. Connell was six foot tall but seemed taller to all who knew him. He was the quiet patriarch of this family. When his time came his coffin was most certainly carried. For a man as respected as he was would have no shortage of pallbearers whenever the day arrived to meet his Maker. He was a man who guided his boys with the gentle space of patience.

He possessed an understated, dry wit. Years ago when an overeager ten-year-old Joseph was in a hurry to get out from the front seat of his father's pickup truck, he pulled so hard on the door handle that it snapped off right in his impatient little hand. As a stunned Joseph looked over at his father, Mr. Connell calmly leaned over, raised the door latch for his son, and said, "Here, let me unlock that for you."

Life was hard enough, the way John Connell figured it. Particularly out here in Montana country. It was an epic landscape to be sure. But that did not diminish the fact that life here required constant vigilance.

He knew that this countryside was as demanding and potentially dangerous as it was beautiful. Most everyone by the age of four knew to never startle a horse nor approach it from behind, lest thousands of years of evolution might cause it to kick its powerful hind legs, and even a half-hearted warning of flying hoofs could do real damage.

Guns were a way of life here and every household had a dozen or more, from a Winchester target rifle that could find its target a thousand feet away to an 1873 Long Colt revolver to smaller handguns that Mr. Connell collected purely out of interest, such as the tiny Derringer pistol. A weapon that was so small it was almost a gun in name only, as it fired only one bullet and could fit in the palm of a man's hand or be otherwise easily hidden.

Both Joseph and Billy had been skilled at shooting since the age of ten. Guns were needed partly for hunting deer and their larger cousin the elk as food to eat. And partly because black bears, mountain lions, or a pack of coyotes might need to hear the blast of a high powered rifle to keep their distance. As such predators would think nothing of stalking a human if hungry enough.

Yet it was the act of sculpting the land that required the most extreme caution, such as something so simple as chopping down a tree. Contrary to what everyone saw in the movies, trees did not fall obediently and predictably to the ground while someone yelled "Timber." That was not how physics worked. For when a tree soaring hundreds of feet on high that weighed up to ten thousand pounds suddenly fell at the speed of gravity in one direction, the thick wood of the just cut trunk flew airborne at unforgiving speed in the opposite direction, easily 'kicking' twenty feet in the air. And if a careless human stood in its path while admiring his handiwork, he would not be for the world much longer.

While a good many dangers could be avoided, some had their own path to carve out. Three years prior their nearest neighbors were two good natured brothers who lived a dozen miles to the north. To a man, woman, and child neighbors in Montana were an unspoken extended family of sorts. There was an etiquette to country living. No one was in a hurry nor rushed anyone else to be either. People were naturally considerate to each other and lending a helping hand was the default inclination toward one another.

As holiday season approached these two brothers had invited a dear friend to visit from Ohio, by train of course. Said friend arrived three days before Christmas. The brothers set off into town twenty-five miles away in their horse drawn sleigh. To greet their friend and bring him back to their home for a month long spell. The heartfelt greeting at the train station went off without much to distinguish it save for the happy holiday cheer.

But the journey home was another matter. A white out descended upon them without warning. An onslaught of heavy snow as thick and furious as it was unrelenting.

All three were found the next morning just five miles from home. Frozen to death along with the horse and partially buried in the snow. And so Mr. Connell instilled in his boys a deep respect for Mother Nature: Enjoy her bounty and beauty but never take her for granted.

The natural head for business that ran through the Connell bloodline did not skip him, but he went about life his own way. Mr. Connell could have followed in his father's and grandfather's footsteps. For as an only child the ranch and its bounty had passed to him. With his keen insight into how to lower the cost of raising cattle and horses for sale – his belief that all of life was the melodic dance of age, genetics, environment, and food – he could have grown the ranch to a thousand head of cattle and a hundred horses. Each animal generating revenue.

But Mr. Connell had another vision for his family. So upon his father's passing he sold off most all of the cattle, save but a few dozen cows now too old for anything but eating grass, while just ten favorite horses had all the Connell acreage to call their own.

It occurred to him that in the boom that followed the end of World War II, both in population and commerce from local to interstate, that folks would be wanting to drink a lot more soda pop in these unfolding times of plenty. And for that they would need bottles from which to glug it back down their turkey wattle. So Mr. Connell opened the first bottling plant in all of Montana. It wasn't long before it was the biggest west of Ohio.

This decision to not monetize the land left the beauty to be a source of joy, not unwavering labor. For a daily gift on this ranch happened every morning, when the rising sun cracked over the horizon and cast a soft calming yellow light upon the mountain tops.

But it was not morning on this Saturday in the spring of 1958.

It was 2:30 in the afternoon and Joseph had yet to emerge for the day.

He finished showering, got dressed, then paused in the opening to his bedroom doorway. Joseph could hear his mother's worry in the form of dishes clanking about her hands in the sink. He forced himself to take the deepest breath he could muster. In a vain effort to banish the affliction that had taken up well-worn residence upon his face. For the dark circles around his eyes were a constant companion that no boy his age should know so intimately.

Joseph entered the kitchen where his mother's presence filled the space like no other. For while society at large was patriarchal in nature, this household was all Bonnie Connell in strength. She had three religions: family, God, and her garden. In that order.

Heaven help anyone who threatened the first.

She was a woman of deep faith and well active in their church, with a particularly close relationship to Pastor David. Bonnie appreciated that he cared authentically and guided but never preached nor condescended nor threatened with eternal damnation. Though he was ten years her junior, still in his mid-thirties, he earned his pulpit and the respect of his flock. He was a family man himself and knew the challenges of simply trying to get through life and all its difficulties with as much gratitude and grace as possible, which often seemed by design to come through adversity.

Mrs. Connell felt God more than somewhere up in Heaven. More than even just in her heart. To her God was everywhere from the rocks to the trees to the air they breathed. Still, she was not the Connell family member with the strongest relationship to God. That distinction belonged to Joseph. Though where her connection was animated by love, his had been curated in a cauldron of despair that had been churned by the alchemy of pain into a deep seeded anger. Though he kept that truth from his family, for he did not wish to upset them.

Joseph walked into the kitchen, poured himself a glass of orange juice and sat down at the table. He was handsome by any measure. With high cheekbones, pale green eyes, and an always messy mop of chestnut brown hair. As a younger boy he had been the mischievous one in the family. Ever since the age of five, when he discovered that shaking his money maker in his tighty whities underpants elicited deep belly laughs from his family. Billy was the brainiac. Easily smart enough to attend some fancy Ivy League university back East on a full scholarship. Even his teachers peppered him to go. But Billy had no need for such things. He had no more desire to ever be away from his beloved home than his parents did.

He was, however, even as a boy enamored with history. Epic events and battles that changed the course of human history. Particularly how empires of days gone by were able to rule far off lands thousands of miles away.

Joseph had little use for history and facts from long ago. He didn't see why he should care what someone else did way back when, since he wasn't there. So, whenever Billy would be given to prattle on at length about this cool fact or fascinating historical story, Joseph would wait patiently until his older brother was distracted by his own excitement, then fall back half a step and oh so innocently insert his foot between his brother's feet mid stride. Without fail, Billy would tumble mid-sentence ass over tea kettle to the ground. Joseph was generally too busy laughing to stop his older brother from rolling him down the hill like a sack of potatoes in playful retribution.

Billy's attempts at mischief were not as successful.

Some years back he thought he had stumbled across the perfect opportunity at his parents' wedding anniversary party. There were so many friends and neighbors who attended it was as busy as any annual county fair. With a good crowd of boys around, Billy tried to tag his little brother with the nickname "Hollywood" because he looked like all those good looking matinee idols at the movie theater. He even tried to enlist the help of surrounding boys by mock acting out a scene from an imaginary movie where the leading man movie star plays kissy-face huggy-bear with the lead actress.

It might have worked too. Except that mid kissy-face, Joseph slapped Billy with the speed of a mongoose and the partially eaten hot dog in his mouth came snorting out his nose. All the boys were laughing until their sides hurt, just not in the way that Billy had envisioned. As usual, Joseph was able to offer little defense through his laughter as his older brother gave him a full complement of wet willies while he straddled his chest.

But those days felt a thousand miles away now.

"Morning, Mom," Joseph said.

Mrs. Connell brought him freshly baked bread and butter.

"It stopped being morning a few hours ago," she replied.

"Sorry."

"I could make you some eggs if you'd like?" she offered with only love in her voice.

"That would be great, thanks."

"Your father shoveled out the stalls for you. Said it was an early birthday present. Maybe you could brush the horses?" She asked.

No horse needed to be brushed. But no horse would ever turn away a person who wanted to brush its coat. It was as near to getting a massage as a horse could get. It was also a meditative act, as beneficial to the human doing the brushing as it was pleasing to the animal.

Joseph knew that more than likely his mother had asked his father to do his chores so that she could orchestrate something that might soothe him. It was just another of the too many reasons to count why he loved his mother so dearly. Even if he was having more and more difficulty in showing it.

"Sure, Mom. I wouldn't mind that at all," he replied affectionately.

After Joseph finished eating he walked down the gravel driveway and headed for the barn. He got about halfway down when his mother's garden fifty yards off in the distance caught his eye. He couldn't quite say why but something wasn't right. He headed toward it.

As it was still mid-May there wasn't too much in the garden that was ready to be picked, save for the lettuce, swiss chard, radishes, and asparagus. The corn, beans, and squash would not be planted until the following week to make sure that a late frost, uncommon but not unheard of, couldn't roll in and freeze the seeds. Just starting to emerge but not mature enough to be picked until late in the summer were peas, beets, onions, and cabbage.

Joseph made his way up to the chicken wire fence that kept out deer and assorted wildlife and there he saw what he had sensed. Never before had he seen his mother's precious garden so overgrown with weeds, nearly choking out the plants she had painstakingly nurtured. And he knew he was the cause. His mother had been so thrown by him of late that she had neglected to care for row after row of food that was her pride and joy in growing.

He entered the garden gate, grabbed an overturned bucket in the corner, got down on his knees and manicured her garden for an hour. Weed by weed, row by row. Until every plant had all the room to breathe it needed and deserved.

After he finished Joseph made his way down to the barn to grab a grooming brush off the shelf. As he reached for it he noticed that a pitchfork had fallen from the hook on the wooden wall from which it hung and laid on the ground. Mr. Connell's *"put everything back in its proper place"* mantra took over without even conscious thought as Joseph reached down, picked it up, and hung it back safely onto the wall.

He made his way into the nearby pen where all ten horses awaited him. Horses were Joseph's refuge from his life and himself. Around them his Herculean efforts to hold his demons at bay were granted a reprieve, however briefly. He simply loved everything about them. From their distinctive smell, a mix of hay, earth, grass, equine sweat and body oil, to the unmistakable sounds they made. The whinny, which was a horse's way of calling out to friends, to the nicker which was a soft, low breathy whinny which meant that a horse wanted you to come closer. Joseph was never the recipient of a snort, an alarm sound that could be dangerous to anyone that made a horse feel threatened.

Horses were majestic creatures from any vantage point. Elegant and powerful animals that could grow to a thousand plus pounds of pure muscle yet still exude refinement as if they were Mother Nature's favorite creation. As an animal of prey, thousands of years of evolution had taught every horse to be wary of any approaching animal or person for fear of becoming dinner. Even after concluding that a human was not there to cause it harm, a horse would not obey a person unless it could be convinced to do so by seeing that person as the herd leader. Horses were herd animals so they naturally looked for a leader.

Young men generation after generation were taught how to convey to a horse that it should obey you: approach it with a fixed, determined gaze. Stiffen your back, pull your shoulders back square and broad, and approach it with confidence.

Joseph did none of that. As he got near the horses his body went soft and relaxed as the tension in his spirit melted away. It only drew the horses to him with more affection. He walked among them as an accepted member of the herd not a leader to be feared nor obeyed. As he made his way around and through them, each nuzzled up against him and offered its nose, hoping to be caressed, which Joseph was only too happy to oblige. As much for his benefit as the small herd of horses.

Happy was by far the most affectionate horse toward him and was selfish with her turn at being brushed. She was the herd leader but that was not why Joseph gave her all the time she desired. Six years ago Mr. Connell had taken his boys to a horse auction in the next county over. It was intended as nothing more than a nice afternoon and an opportunity to show them how a horse auction worked, not much different than how their great-great-grandfather, Tobias Connell, got his start selling wild horses to the U.S. Cavalry after he had trained them.

But not everything goes according to plan in life and this was no exception. A full sized mare had been spooked. No one could say why, but everyone could sure see what was happening with their own two eyes. She refused to leave the pen nor let anyone near her, as she bucked and reared up violently with front hoofs flying at anyone who dared approach her. Three grown men had been chased out in quick order. It seemed that in a very short amount of time this problem was going to be resolved with a bullet to her skull. There wasn't much else anyone could think to do.

Eleven-year-old Joseph had no intention of allowing that solution. He slipped passed his father and brother and before anyone could do anything about it, there stood Joseph a mere ten feet from the snorting, angry, scared, and dangerous animal. The mare went back to what had worked that day. She reared up and threatened with flying front hoofs. Billy instinctively moved to grab Joseph and bring him back to safety.

But Mr. Connell took hold of his oldest boy by the collar to give Joseph a chance. He could see that there were by now a dozen rifles fixed on the animal. Mr. Connell had been hunting with each ranch hand who now had the horse's skull dead center in their crosshairs and he knew, to a man, each was an expert marksman. His boy was not in any real danger though Joseph didn't know that. Mr. Connell was more concerned for his son's emotional well-being if this ended poorly.

Joseph stood his ground. Not with aggression. Not with posture or tactics. He simply stood in front of this animal who was frightened and lashing out in anger. Standing still was no guarantee of safety though, for an angry horse might very well charge and knock a person to the ground with enough force to kill. But the longer Joseph stood there without reacting to the horse's threats, the more the horse could read his energy and intentions. And slowly, very slowly, the horse's breathing calmed. Its heart rate slowed. Eventually it stopped snorting and kicking.

Still Joseph did not move near nor away. He held out his left hand, palm up. No treats. No carrots. Just an empty hand in offering. The horse raised and lowered its head, not sure what to make of this young boy. Still Joseph waited. Hand extended. After pawing at the dirt several times, the horse slowly walked to him. She sniffed his hand and body. And finally, finally, she nuzzled up against him.

No bullet needed to be wasted that day. Mr. Connell bought the horse and brought her home. Joseph named her Happy.

He brushed the coat of each horse with tenderness and affection. Nintely minutes later it was time to get to work. He returned the brush to the shelf he had found it on and headed up to the second story of the barn, where all of his fighting equipment awaited him.

Homemade swords were carved from Ponderosa pine so that he could re-enact the battles of his nightmares and visions to see how he might fare better the next time, as there was always going to be a next time. He used a heavy bag for kicking that hung from the rafters, a speed bag for hand eye coordination, and weights for packing on as much muscle as his lean athletic frame would accommodate. Today's workout was just a warmup for later.

As Joseph went through his workout routine, Billy pulled up in his mud strewn pickup truck. Like all young men in Montana he had been driving legally since he was fifteen, competently since thirteen, and decently since age eleven. His favorite song played on the radio and he sang along, well out of tune as he couldn't catch a beat

Grandpa didn't fight in World War One. There isn't even a war going on right now," Billy said.

But there was a war going on. Just not one Billy could see.

"I just… I can't… I can't stay," Joseph admitted.

If he could have chosen any place on earth to be born it was right here: the gorgeous Montana countryside to breathe in while sitting atop a galloping horse. Joseph didn't want to leave his family. It broke his heart. But he was afraid that if he stayed, the way he was deteriorating from within, he didn't know how much longer he could go on. Though he couldn't tell any of this to his older brother.

"You were the youngest supervisor in the history of the plant," Joseph offered.

Billy looked at his little brother square in the eyes and the love that he felt for him caused his frustration to melt.

"Yeah, listen, Joey. Mom… your T-shirt again. What's–" he started to ask before Joseph cut him off.

"Nothing," he lied. "Hit myself training."

"While you were sleeping?" Billy pressed.

"Forgot to change before going to bed," Joseph dug in.

"Sure. Right. Joey…"

"Remember that time we stole a hundred bottles from the plant and used them for target practice?" Joseph asked to redirect the conversation.

Billy stared at him a moment, then complied.

"Never seen Dad so mad. Still don't know what he was more cross about. Us shooting up a hundred perfectly good bottles," Billy said.

"Or taking his shotgun without permission," Joseph finished.

"Yeah, and you said to the foreman, 'Shut up and give me the bottles. My dad owns the place.' I swear, if you were a foot taller he'd a cracked you good."

"I thought he was going to for sure," Joseph reminisced.

They walked back toward the house.

"Well, little brother, tomorrow is your eighteenth birthday and you'll be a man. 12:18 am to be exact, I believe?" Billy asked.

"Yeah," Joseph replied.

He was unaware that Billy and his parents had no intention of letting him go without a fight, and that included some well planned out loving manipulation. Billy and their father had commissioned the most decorated saddlemaker in all of Montana to handcraft Joseph a Western saddle of such intoxicating and sumptuous leather glory that, they hoped, no one including Joseph could resist its charm. Knowing as they did how his love for horses ran so deep, perhaps they could coax him into postponing his volunteer enlistment in the Army. Mr. and Mrs. Connell had refused Joseph's request that they sign the waiver to allow him to enlist while still only seventeen years old.

In case the one-of-a-kind saddle wasn't enough, Mrs. Connell had also commissioned a pair of custom riding boots for Joseph. They took three months to make starting with the stacked cowhide leather dyed a deep and rich burgundy, which was his favorite color. She had brought to the bootmaker a pair of Joseph's old boots to use as a guide, to custom cut the rounded toe and high shaft for his muscular calf muscles. On both sides starting at the ankle and weaving its way up to the top of the boot was a crest of a shield that Joseph had drawn as a small boy.

It took painstaking skill and patience on the part of the bootmaker to hand stitch the crest in the exact design that Joseph had drawn. It was a shield with two crisscrossing swords on it. The swords had a distinctive grip capped by an ivory tip. He had charged Mrs. Connell triple his normal rate, which she was only too happy to pay with gratitude. She would have paid a hundred times his artisan price if these cowboy boots would make Joseph want to stay with them on the ranch. Even for just another year perhaps.

Whether the custom presents plan was successful or not, either way it was the end of an era. Both Connell boys as of tomorrow would now be men. In the eyes of the world and God. And the protections life bathed a boy in until he reached manhood would be withdrawn. As were the natural biorhythms to be adhered to by all.

Billy put his arm around Joseph.

"Couple of hours from now, Joey, you won't be a boy anymore. You can do whatever you want in life. And whatever you choose, I'll support you," Billy said.

"Thanks, Billy," Joseph replied.

"Hey, guess what? Lily's pregnant."

Joseph's face brightened at the news and a big smile came across his face. The biggest Billy had seen in quite some time.

"We're naming him James," he continued.

"Well, how do you know it's going to be a boy?" Joseph asked.

"How do I know it's? Why, you know there hasn't been a girl born to the Connell family since The Middle Ages because of the extra high iron in our blood," Billy answered.

Joseph laughed but managed to reply, "You couldn't even tell me what centuries The Middle Ages were, even though you are a history aficionado."

"After The Early Ages," Billy replied.

"And before The Late Ages, no doubt?" Joseph peppered him.

"Yeah, well," laughed Billy. "I suppose you got a better explanation?"

"No, but I wouldn't mind having a girl someday."

"You?! Sorry, little brother, but you need a wife for such things and you haven't even had a girlfriend since Hollie. And that was…" Billy trailed off trying to remember the year.

"Yeah, yeah, I know when that was. I'm just saying," Joseph countered.

"Save it. When you're seventy and alone and I've got grandkids I don't want you blaming me," Billy smiled.

"I won't be alone," Joseph said in mock protest.

"Come on, Lily's on her way over and Dad should be home soon. Let's see what Mom's got for dinner."

Joseph stopped walking.

"Can't. Got the tournament tonight," he replied.

Billy turned around.

With unparalleled physical gifts Joseph could have been a champion rodeo rider, equestrian, or wrestler even. But he was never seeking attention nor to belong to a group of companions nor even praise of any kind. And yet since the age of thirteen he had been the Pacific Northwest Adult Division Karate Champion, besting men two, even three times his age. He did not compete for love of sport nor accomplishment. He had never even brought a single trophy home in all the years his legend grew. But nearest Billy could figure, it was his only known coping mechanism.

"Skip it, Joey. Have dinner and then… come to church. There's a special Midnight Mass tonight," he coaxed.

"Midnight Mass? Tonight?" Joseph asked.

Joseph had not been to church since he was ten years old. His last time sitting in the pews with his brother and parents had been the time that Pastor David had given a sermon on how much God loved all of his children. No matter what they did and no matter what befell them, he never stopped loving them. When the Sunday Service ended Pastor David stood at the door, smiled in earnest and affectionately shook hands with each parishioner, young and old, as they exited the church.

Joseph sat in his pew until he was the last to exit. His parents waited for him just outside the doors, standing next to Pastor David. Joseph quietly made his way down the aisle, walked to Pastor David, looked up at him and said, "I don't believe you."

After that day neither Mr. nor Mrs. Connell could convince Joseph to return to church and they chose to not force him.

"Yeah, Pastor David said something about feeling like we all need to be in church with him tonight," Billy replied.

"Oh."

"Come with, Joey. It's been so long you may not even remember what the place looks like."

"Can't," Joseph stood firm.

"Okay," Billy sighed in defeat.

CHAPTER 2

Hours later Joseph stood alone among hundreds of martial arts competitors at the annual Pacific Northwest Karate Championships. All except one who had been there to fight that day were dressed in traditional martial arts uniforms of either white or black, depending on which school they belonged to and the historical lineage of their fighting style. They were of assorted rank from the beginner white belt to expert black belt.

Joseph, however, did not have on a uniform as he did not belong to any karate school. He stood barefoot in an old T-shirt and even older sweatpants. Except for the eight ounce fighting gloves on his hands he could have looked as if he were dressed for a lazy and relaxed Sunday afternoon.

But this night swirled with forces whose power Joseph did not yet know intimately.

Most competitors had arrived with their karate teacher to advise them in competition. All the black belts had lost except for two: Joseph, who had no teacher, and the man he was about to fight for the Championship, Tom. Joseph waited patiently for his match against his thirty-year-old opponent. He had never fought him before, nor heard of him, but Tom was also undefeated and had traveled up from California specifically to test his mettle against this boy phenom he had heard so much about.

Tom stood a formidable six feet six inches tall and towered over the otherwise sturdy five foot ten inch Joseph, so his longer limbs would undeniably give him a reach advantage. Joseph was untroubled. He had fought warriors more imposing than Tom, though if he ever told anyone where they would not believe him and might even try to have him committed to an asylum.

Though this was the Championship match it was still a no frills organization so the field of battle consisted of a twenty foot square in the middle of the auditorium marked off with thick black tape. Dozens of defeated black belts stood around the perimeter and eagerly awaited the fight as much as the hundreds of fans in the bleachers. Tom warmed up and strategized with his teacher across from Joseph, who stood and waited quietly.

They couldn't begin until the referee made his way down to the field of battle. He had been the champion of his day but was now in his mid-fifties and well beyond fighting age. Though he still cut a commanding presence and was well respected.

Tom did his best to eyeball Joseph and try to get in his head. But he might as well have been trying to scare a longhorn steer for all the good it would do him. As Joseph ignored his opponent's attempts at psychological warfare, a soft spoken sixteen-year-old boy named Mike approached him. Mike was a black belt and they knew each other from school. They were not friends, though not through any defect in Mike. Joseph did not have any friends.

"Joe?" Mike called to him.

Joseph couldn't hear him over the noise of the crowd and nearby competitors talking.

"Joe?" Mike called louder.

Joseph turned and saw him.

"Hey, Mike, how are you?" Joseph asked.

"Good, I'm good. Sorry to bother you so close to your fight."

Not far away, but purposefully hidden from Joseph's field of vision, stood Lahiri. He was an elderly Hindu monk from India, diminutive in stature. Though his country had been known for a thousand years for producing the world's finest fabrics of silk and cotton in an endless variety of vibrant colors, he stood in a simple brown cloth garment he had made himself. Spun upon a wooden handloom that he had built. While this humble man had originally stood a modest five feet, eight inches tall, he had been shrunken by time and now stood five feet, four inches.

Though he once had a thick head of hair, he had long outlived such fleeting possessions. But no matter for his bald head only added to his humble presence of dignity and grace. Compassion undiminished by time gleamed in his eyes and kindness was etched upon his face.

He had traveled a great distance and had waited a very long time for this night to arrive.

Mike continued, "I was just wondering, um, I was just wondering, if you, I'm fighting tomorrow for the Under Eighteen title, and I was hoping you might have some advice for me?"

"Sure, Mike. You're fighting Fred. He's tough," Joseph said.

"Tell me about it," Mike replied.

"And you want to know how to defeat him?" Joseph asked in a reassuring voice.

"Very much," Mike answered eagerly.

"Well, he's got fists that feel like bricks, a hard right jab and a wicked left hook. Almost beat me once when we were ten years old," Joseph offered.

"Yeah, he still talks about that too. Claims no one has ever come that close to beating you," Mike said.

Joseph smiled. "He's right. I was seeing Tweety Birds for a while there. Tell you what, his left side defense is weak. You stay out of range from his punches and hit him with a right roundhouse kick, he'll go down like a sack of potatoes and not get back up."

A distressed look came across Mike's face.

"But, but, I can't. My right hamstring is hurt," he shared.

"I know it is, Mike. Every fighter here knows it is, including Fred."

"But if I try that, I could tear it," said Mike fearfully.

"You probably will. Which is why Fred will never expect you to throw it. Listen, you can limp out of here in defeat tomorrow or be carried out in victory," Joseph said.

"Right, right," Mike tried to convince himself, but still very much uncertain.

"You have to decide if your actions are worth the cost. It is that simple," Joseph counseled.

Those last words cut into Lahiri as he momentarily looked down.

"Thanks, Joe. I really appreciate you helping me and sorry again for bothering you so close to your championship fight."

"No problem, Mike. Good luck tomorrow, whatever you decide to do."

"You too, not that you'll need any luck," Mike joked.

Joseph looked over at Tom and said, "Never know. Big fella' looks like he wants that scrap metal trophy real bad."

Mike smiled, nodded, and walked away favoring his injured leg.

The referee made his way down to Joseph and Tom, which brought the crowd to life with cheers and foot stomping.

Over the loudspeaker the announcer further whipped up the crowd. He first introduced the formidable challenger, Tom, and played up how this would be an epic battle of wills between two determined warriors where only one could be the victor. Joseph didn't like that the announcer made him sound like some comic book character, whose mettle would be tested after being a local phenom who had defeated men two, three times his age since he was just a young buck of thirteen.

The referee walked to the center of the square and motioned for Joseph and Tom to join him, which they did. He then addressed the fighters.

But before he spoke, Lahiri closed his eyes in concentration and hijacked Joseph's consciousness onto the astral plane. A non-physical energy field that co-existed with physical reality.

It was hidden to most. But not to all.

Most experienced it voluntarily after decades of dedicated spiritual effort. Joseph was not given the choice. Most found it a healing and nurturing place of celestial energies. Joseph did not.

He stood in front of Tom and the referee with a far off look in his eyes as he tried to function in both the physical world and on the all too familiar to him astral plane. He had years of experience in trying to navigate them at the same time.

But never, never during a karate tournament. And this scared him mightily.

Dressed in an animal hide around his hips as he wielded a sword, Joseph ran barefoot through a forest barely illuminated by moonlight. The sword had a tempered blade of high carbon steel with a grip of wood surrounded by a brass hand covering. The wood handle was overlaid in leather with a twisted copper wire for grip assurance.

Sweat poured from his brow as fog rolled in and made it harder for him to find his way. He jumped over a fallen tree and looked over his shoulder for his pursuers that he knew were not far behind. Three seven foot tall warriors, exact replicas of each other. No head or body hair and clothed as he was.

Though their hands were empty of weapon, still it was they who pursued him. Joseph labored to breathe and run faster.

"Okay, fellas," the referee began. "You both know the rules but let's review them anyway. No shots to the groin or kneecaps. Obey my commands at all times. When a point is scored you will both return to your corners. Is that understood?"

Tom nodded. Joseph was unresponsive.

He came to a clearing and stopped. He looked back, but no sign of the three warriors.

"Joe?" the referee said.

Still no response.

"Mr. Connell," the referee inquired more forcefully.

Still no response.

Joseph's chest heaved to take in more air as he surveyed the terrain. But not for long. The three warriors, whom he had just so exhaustedly outrun, reappeared a mere five feet in front of him. But now, each held a double-edged sword that glistened in the tormenting light.

"Boy! I'm talking to you," the annoyed referee ramped up his tone.

Joseph managed a nod.

The referee stepped back and yelled, "Fight!"

The crowd roared. Tom and Joseph stalked their way toward each other, as Joseph struggled to focus on the physical and astral planes simultaneously.

Lahiri remained seated. His eyes closed. Very much concentrated of effort.

Tom was surprised by Joseph's sluggish engagement and quickly seized upon the moment by smashing him in the forehead with an overhead heel kick. The blow landed unblocked and catapulted Joseph off of his feet and back into the fighters who surrounded them. The crowd was stunned. No one had ever seen Joseph struck so cleanly and so forcefully.

A large welt immediately formed on his forehead. He was disoriented but got back to his feet, though now suffering from a severe concussion as his brain had been slammed violently into his skull when his head snapped back from the blow. The fight should have been stopped then and there.

The three warriors slowly stalked their way toward Joseph, encircling him. The first warrior to his left attacked with a two-handed overhead strike with his sword. Joseph deflected the attack, spun into a spinning back kick, and smashed his foot hard in the man's abdomen, knocking him to the ground.

The referee walked to Joseph, concerned by how fast the welt continued to swell up in size.

"Looks pretty bad to me, son. You want to quit?" he asked.

Joseph shook his head, concealing the fact that speaking coherently in the moment would have been difficult.

"Suit yourself. You're the champion," the referee said.

He raised his right hand and awarded the point to Tom. He motioned for both fighters to return to their starting positions, then yelled, "Fight!"

Joseph and Tom both came out with aggression but every flying fist, knee, and elbow thrown in close quarters was blocked. Everyone in the auditorium was on their feet screaming. Everyone except the quiet and concentrating Lahiri.

Joseph retreated a half step back. Tom took the bait and moved in, only to eat a powerful left roundhouse kick to the side of his head. He stumbled back on wobbly legs. Joseph charged in for the finish, but Tom had just enough space to land a quick kick flush to his midsection, breaking Joseph's ribs on the right side.

He crumbled to the floor.

"That's it!" the referee yelled above the deafening screams of the crowd.

Fighters mobbed Tom. It wasn't that they were happy to see Joseph defeated. They just couldn't believe what they had witnessed.

The old man from India relaxed his efforts and opened his eyes.

The referee helped the injured Joseph to his feet and into the nearby locker room. He carefully sat him down on a splintered wooden bench, as Joseph winced in agony.

"I've seen many a broken ribs in my life, boy, and those are busted up good. The less you try to breathe, the less it will hurt," the referee offered.

Joseph tried to smile in gratitude.

"Crowd is dispersing. I'll keep the fans out. I expect you don't want to talk with anyone right about now. Fight doctor should be here any minute."

Joseph nodded.

"You were bound to lose someday, son. Everyone does. Just the way life works. You're still the best damn fighter I've ever seen," the referee complimented him.

"Thank you," Joseph whispered.

"Now don't go trying to talk, you jackass. Save your breath."

Joseph nodded again.

"I have been around thousands of fighters in my day. And all my decades of experience in the fight game tells me, I don't expect we'll be seeing you again. Don't think you enjoy fighting. Can't say I even know why you been doing it," the referee shared.

Joseph offered a genuine smile.

The referee headed out of the locker room. As he got to the door he noticed a dozen fans trying to look in.

"Get your asses out of here," he scolded them.

The fans scurried away and the crowd filed out of the building, all still talking about the most exciting and unexpected fight they had ever witnessed. The fight doctor made his way in to see Joseph. He was a soft spoken man in his sixties who didn't approve of fighting, but volunteered his time to make sure any injuries would not go untreated.

He pulled out a pair of scissors and cut Joseph's T-shirt off of him to inspect the injured area, which by now was a mess of black and blue and swollen patches of discolored yellow skin.

"Sure enough your ribs are broken. At least four. Maybe five or six. Hard to say without an x-ray. This is going to hurt but I need to make sure no fragments have moved," the doctor said.

Joseph winced as the doctor felt around his rib cage as gently as he could.

"Sorry about this, boy," he offered.

"It's okay," Joseph responded.

A quick inspection confirmed for the doctor what he already knew.

"Well, the good news if you can call it that, is that yes they are broken but no, there is nothing to do but let them heal. I can wrap them if you'd like?"

Joseph shook his head.

"Okay, then. No strenuous activity for six weeks. Deep breathing likely won't be your friend for a while, nor will be trying to sit back up if you lay down. I recommend you sleep sitting up for at least two weeks."

Joseph nodded.

The doctor reached into his black medical bag and retrieved a bottle of pills.

"No pills," Joseph said.

"When your adrenaline wears off, those busted ribs are going to feel like you're getting stabbed with spears. From the *inside*," the doctor informed him.

"No pills."

"It's just a little something for the pain. Not like you'll get addicted from one dose."

Joseph shook his head firmly.

"Your call. You want me to get someone to drive you home?"

Joseph labored to breathe through the pain.

"No, Sir. But thank you. No need to wrap them either," he said.

"Okay, son. If you change your mind, I'll be around for another thirty minutes or so," the doctor offered, then walked out of the locker room. Leaving Joseph alone with his thoughts and painfully broken ribs.

Outside in the woods was a deer unlike any other. Deer in these parts were not migratory, never venturing far from where they had been born. This particular animal had never been born. Deer at this time of year as spring was unfolding had no antlers to speak of. Only little nubs atop their head from the winter. Antlers would grow slowly as the weather warmed through the summer and not be full sized until fall was on the horizon.

This deer, however, had a full thicket of regal antlers, as there may be business to attend to this night. This creature had never known the pangs of hunger nor the urge to procreate. Save for the blinking of its eyes, it stood statue stiff. And waited.

Back in the locker room Joseph sat on the wooden bench and labored to find the sweet spot of limited breathing that gave him enough air, but not deep enough to cause excruciating pain every time his lungs filled and emptied.

Lahiri walked silently into the locker room, creating not a sound of disturbance. Joseph did not notice him at first, busy as he was looking for the keys to his pickup truck. Lahiri looked up at the clock on the wall.

The time read midnight.

He then stared at a pink jagged shaped birthmark just below Joseph's solar plexus.

The deer in the woods lowered its head slightly, squinted its eyes, and listened. A moment later Joseph noticed

Lahiri standing there. He wasn't sure of what to make of this little man from India who smiled kindly at him.

Back in the safety of church Joseph's family sat with other congregation members as Pastor David recited his special Midnight Mass.

"In the land Uz there was a blameless and upright man named Job. In response to Job's plea that he be allowed to see God and hear from him the cause of his suffering, God answers not by justifying his actions before man, but by referring to his omniscience and almighty power."

In the locker room, it was time to make the introduction.

"Hello, Joseph," said Lahiri.

"How did you know my name?" Joseph asked curiously.

Lahiri looked up and pointed at the ceiling. In confusion Joseph looked up too though he wasn't sure what he was supposed to be looking at.

"Announcer told me over the loudspeaker," Lahiri replied with a grin.

"Oh, right," Joseph answered.

"I believe I could be of assistance to you," Lahiri offered.

Joseph stared at him curiously for a moment, but then replied…

"No thank you, Sir. A little ice and I'll be okay."

Lahiri did not move. Joseph looked down, found his keys, grabbed them, then looked back up to see the old man still standing there. He offered this strange visitor another smile. After a moment the old man turned to leave the locker room. When he reached the doorway, he stopped and turned back around. Then said...

"Each must travel the path laid bare."

Joseph heard him but it didn't register. Lahiri turned and exited the locker room.

The deer in the woods dug its powerful hoofs into the earth and took off racing through the trees, snorting like a charging war horse. It had much ground to cover and not a lot of time to do so. Fallen branches crackled beneath its heavy and determined hoofs.

Joseph exited the auditorium and walked gingerly to his pickup truck. Though in great pain he managed to lift himself up on to the seat and carefully began the drive home.

His watch on the front seat showed the time: 12:07 am.

The deer continued its race through the forest. High up on a ridge was a mountain lion. This big cat weighed only two hundred pounds but was such a skilled killing machine that it could take down a thousand pound elk without risk of injury.

It was a master at using its environment as camouflage, though the deer knew of its presence. As a top of the food chain predator this mountain lion could bound forty feet while running, leap fifteen feet in the air, and reach a running speed of fifty miles per hour. None of those abilities appeared necessary though, as this deer raced straight into its path. Even after it had come out well into the open.

The mountain lion was hungry. This deer would make an easy and much needed meal. It ran straight for its prey and with each passing stride the big cat was certain that any evasive maneuver the deer might take would be in vain. It took none. With only fifty yards separating them the mountain lion increased its speed for the kill about to unfold.

Yet as the distance between them erased it was the mountain lion who yielded and in confusion crept closer to the determined deer, who also slowed to a momentary crawl. The predator sensed unfamiliar danger and proceeded with caution.

Until they were face to face. The mountain lion bared its fangs that could rip through flesh with ease. The deer grew impatient. It leaned in closer, an inch from the big cat who came to kill it. It blinked its big brown eyes that conveyed a final warning: depart or be mortally gored. The mountain lion closed its mouth, retreated in fear, and took off running from whence it came.

The deer now had lost time to make up. It taxed its lungs to lethal capacity to reach its goal as it stalked Joseph through the trees, who drove carefully and was happy he was only five minutes from home. He came upon a stretch of familiar roadway. One that he had driven hundreds of times before. It was quiet and straight and peaceful.

And it was here that the deer jumped out from the trees and ran down the center of the road. Headlong into the path of Joseph's oncoming pickup truck.

The time on Joseph's watch read: 12:18 am.

Joseph saw the deer and was immediately alarmed.

This deer should not have antlers yet. But it did.

It should not be running straight at him. But it was.

He slammed on the horn to scare it away. It was not scared.

His bloodstream quickly flooded with adrenaline and his heart raced. He swerved his pickup truck to the right so that he could catch the animal on the corner of his bumper and it would be flicked off the road.

The deer mirrored his adjustment.

He swerved back to the left, desperate to avoid a direct hit.

The deer mirrored him again.

Joseph's world class reflexes were proving to be a problem. A third evasive maneuver by him and he just might avert his anointed date with destiny. Such could not be permitted. So, additional measures were taken.

An unbroken rib on his left side suddenly snapped in two without apparent cause and sent excruciating pain throughout his body. Joseph instinctively let go of the steering wheel with his left hand to clutch at the new stabbing pain.

And a blinding burst of White Light appeared in front of his pickup truck, rendering him unable to see the road. It also provided perfect cover for the determined creature.

The deer kept coming full bore. Through the White Light.

It lowered its head for impact. Joseph's pickup truck smashed head on into the deer. The violent collision caused the animal to fly up onto the hood and then clear over the top of his vehicle. It landed hard in a ditch twenty yards behind him. Joseph's truck careened off the road and into a nearby tree, the largest in the forest.

Metal violently crunched all around as he was catapulted over the steering wheel and through the windshield. Shards of jagged flying glass cut into his now disfigured face. As he flew out of the pickup truck his own body was weaponized against him: the bones of his sternum were snapped like kindling. Jagged fragments punctured the spongy tissue of his lungs repeatedly without mercy. Where a moment ago there was air in his lungs, blood now rushed in and greedily took its place.

Joseph flew through the air defenseless and over the hood of his pickup truck. He smashed face first into the trunk of the tree. His neck was savagely broken. So brutally that he was internally decapitated, where his skull was no longer attached to his spinal column. It was only his shredded yet still loyal neck muscles, the tendons that refused to tear, and a few critical intact nerves that kept his head attached to his broken body.

Still in church, his family sang a hymn along with Father David and their fellow congregants.

Steam spewed from the crumpled radiator as Joseph lay on the ground very near to death.

Lahiri, who had watched the horrific event unfold, calmly walked out from the trees. He first walked to the mortally wounded deer and kneeled beside it. The creature struggled to breathe and looked up at him.

He placed his hand on its heaving chest.

"Thank you, my friend. It is time now for you to rest," he said.

The deer took its last breath, then died.

Lahiri rose and walked to the mangled body of Joseph, whose head rested grotesquely on his left shoulder. His face was mauled flesh. He tenderly lifted Joseph's head from his shoulder and rested it back on the ground in line with his body. Then studied the pink jagged shaped birthmark that had so captivatingly caught his eye back in the locker room. Moments ticked by.

Joseph's Spirit began to depart his body from his chest.

Lahiri placed his hands upon Joseph's ribs. His fingertips then glowed with small illuminations of White Light. Joseph's Spirit was prevented from leaving his body.

It turned to Lahiri.

"Please let me go," his Spirit implored, desperate for this nightmare to be over.

"I cannot," Lahiri replied.

"But I am tired," answered Joseph's Spirit.

Lahiri offered a sad smile of sympathy.

"So am I," he said.

He closed his eyes and concentrated. Blood ceased its determined flow from Joseph's ears, nose, and mouth.

His Spirit was forced back into his body.

Lahiri lovingly caressed Joseph's blood stained forehead. He then rose and walked silently down the road until he came upon a pay phone. He dialed zero for the operator and patiently waited for her to answer. When she did he said, "There has been a most terrible accident. A boy… a man has been badly hurt. Please send an ambulance to Wicker Road just north of Stables Lane."

He then hung up the phone and retreated back into the woods.

CHAPTER 3

An ambulance with lights flashing and siren blaring pulled up to the accident scene fifteen minutes later. The two paramedics, Greg and Cody, were good friends of Billy's from high school and had known Joseph all of his life. Greg was the driver while Cody looked out for the accident scene from the front passenger seat. He saw the smashed pickup truck and told Greg to pull up next to it.

Both young men could see that this was bad. As they exited their ambulance cab it was Greg who first noticed a body. When they ran over to assess the situation it was Cody who recognized the pickup truck.

"That's Joe's truck," he said fearfully.

A moment later they both looked down at the mangled body before them. The ground that Joseph lay upon was uneven and his head had fallen back toward his shoulder. It was a terrifying sight and, even for these experienced paramedics, an overwhelming one. They had seen their fair share of accident victims, even ones who didn't survive. But nothing in their nineteen years had prepared them for this.

Cody turned away, doubled over, and vomited profusely.

Greg ran back to the ambulance and grabbed the backboard. It was heavy and meant to be carried by two paramedics, but Cody was of no help. A tear ran down Greg's cheek as he struggled but summoned the strength to carry the backboard over to Joseph and lay it down near his body. He reached down to Joseph's wrist and felt for a sign of life.

"Cody! Cody! He's got a pulse. Get down here and help me!" Greg shouted.

Cody stopped wretching and straightened up but stared down at Greg as he knelt over the body.

"Get down here," Greg repeated.

"No," Cody whispered as he wiped vomit from his mouth.

"What?!" a stunned Greg replied.

"No. If we move him it'll kill him," Cody said back.

Greg was enraged. He stood up, violently grabbed his friend by the collar, and slammed him up against the tree. Tears streamed down Greg's cheeks. He tried to speak coherently.

"You listen to me, Cody," Greg said.

He slammed his friend up against the tree again.

"I am not! Not! Telling Billy we let his kid brother die out here in the woods because we were too scared to do our jobs," Greg said.

But then softened.

"Now, please, please, get your ass down here and help me," he begged.

Cody nodded.

They both scrambled back down to the ground next to Joseph. Greg reached for his head while Cody held the neck brace. He started to move it back in line with his body so that Cody could wrap the neck brace around him.

But hesitated.

"Do it. We have no choice," Cody reassured him.

They strapped their dear friend's little brother to the backboard, loaded him into the ambulance, and raced toward the hospital.

Not far away, Lahir knelt by a stream and washed Joseph's blood from his hands.

CHAPTER 4

The surgeon looked down at Joseph and could not believe this boy was still alive. He was a competent doctor. Skilled even. But Joseph was a disfigured mass of bloody pulp and the sight of this poor boy who lay on his operating table shook him. He didn't even know where to begin. The four doctors who assisted him and the six nurses all waited for him to give orders. In what seemed like an hour but had only been a minute, he finally led his team. He first turned to the head nurse.

"Amanda, tell the orthopedic team to be on standby to set I don't even know how many broken bones with Series 2 Rods. But they will have to wait to see if we can keep him alive long enough to reduce the swelling in his brain before he strokes out," he said.

Amanda nodded. The surgeon looked at the faces of his team and he could see that he needed to do a better job of leading them in the difficult tasks before them. Labors that would take many hours.

"This boy is counting on us and we are not going to fail him," he said to rally his team.

He then turned to the doctor to his left.

"Tim, we're running out of blood and plasma won't cut it. He's leaking like a sieve," he said.

Amanda spoke up.

"Doctor, there's a line of two, maybe three hundred people outside all waiting to give blood for him," she said.

As soon as Cody and Greg had dropped Joseph off at the Emergency Room doors they raced from house to house. Starting with Billy, who collected his pregnant wife and picked up Mr. and Mrs. Connell. From Billy's house Greg called everyone in the county south of Wicker Road, while Cody drove to the Connell ranch to use their phone and called everyone north of it.

Every member of this humble surgical team was touched.

"Okay, tell all of the O-negative people to form one line and we'll use their blood first. Tell the rest to please form another line and they can still donate to the hospital," the surgeon said.

Amanda exited the operating room to relay the message. Now it was time to get to work.

"Well," the surgeon began, "I don't like to impose my beliefs on others. But I think it's safe to say, if you don't believe in God yet, now might be a good time to start."

Sixteen hours of non-stop surgery later the entire medical team was exhausted and dripping in sweat. But Joseph was miraculously still alive, though for how much longer was anyone's guess.

The surgeon came out to give Joseph's family an update. Paster David kept them company. As soon as he pushed through the doors from the surgical area all of the Connell family stood, desperate for news. Mr. Connell, Billy, and Lily unconsciously stood just a half step behind Mrs. Connell as he approached. It was clear to the surgeon that she was the pillar of the family whom he was to address.

He stood in front of her and began to speak, but was overcome with exhaustion and emotion and he cried right in front of Joseph's mother. It wasn't uncontrollable crying or wailing, it was simply a human response to the hours upon hours of trying to put her boy back together and now having to face her with the news. He turned his head to the side and put his hand to his face. Tears streamed down Mr. Connell's face, as they did with Billy and Lily. Pastor David put his arm around Mrs. Connell. But she was not going to fall apart. Not while Joey needed her.

Mrs. Connell put a comforting hand upon the surgeon's elbow. He turned and looked at her with gratitude, then took a deep breath and resumed his duty.

"Mrs. Connell, we were able to repair the damage to his internal organs as well as can be expected. His neck is broken and he has suffered an internal decapitation, where his skull has broken away from his spinal column," he said.

"Today is his birthday," Mrs. Connell replied.

The surgeon was unsure what to make of her reply. Was she in shock? he wondered.

"Miraculously, not all of the nerves in his neck were severed. We have removed the back portion of his skull to relieve the pressure on his brain, but he has slipped into a coma," he continued.

"For how long?" Mr. Connell asked.

"There is no way to know. But, Mr. and Mrs. Connell, I have to be honest with you. I have no medical explanation for why your son is still alive. I do not deem to know the workings of Divine Providence, but his ruptured aorta alone should have killed him long before he arrived here for treatment. All I mean to say is, if he were my boy, I would say my goodbyes while I still had the chance. I am sorry. All we can do now is pray," he replied.

Mrs. Connell thanked the surgeon, then led her family and Pastor David into Joseph's hospital room.

The assorted machines keeping him alive had a macabre rhythm, sustaining life but also daggers in the form of sound. He lay in bed with his head encased in a metal halo of spikes drilled directly into his skull. The halo kept his head from moving even a millimeter until his broken neck healed, if he lived that long. His teeth had all been knocked out when his face hit the tree and though his broken jaw had been wired shut, his mouth looked disfigured with no teeth to give it a familiar shape. His eyes were grotesquely swollen shut. Crisscrossing opaque sutures took up real estate on his face.

Mrs. Connell walked up to the near side of his bed as Mr. Connell, Billy, and Lily stood beside her. Pastor David walked to the other side. His mother, with the most tender of love leaned down and gently kissed his once handsome face.

Then she spoke to her boy, "You will not leave us, Joey. I declare this for all to hear."

As she rose back to stand upright, a lone rogue tear escaped from the corner of her left eye. She looked Pastor David square in the eyes. He nodded.

Joseph did survive the night. And the night after that. Six months after his accident he was still very much alive and the scars that outlined his face seemed to fade a bit. He remained in a coma and was medically designated as being in a vegetative state with no expected chance of regaining consciousness, though this did not deter his family in the slightest. There was still brain activity as tests demonstrated, but there had been so much damage, the surgeon felt it would have been immoral to give his family hope. But he did not know the Connell clan.

The only blessing to Joseph being in a prolonged coma was that he was not awake to feel the needles, the surgeries, the endless cuts to his flesh to repair his face and body as best as the surgeons could, which was not unimpressive. At last count Joseph had undergone fifteen reconstructive surgeries. And for each and every one his family was there to see him off to surgery and to welcome him back when it was complete. Speaking to him each time as if he were awake and could hear them, as they believed he could.

They visited him daily without fail. Sometimes together on weekends and on shifts during the week. This

Tuesday afternoon it was Billy who sat with him and held his little brother's hand.

"Come on, Joey. I've seen you take worse shots than this," Billy said. "Remember when you were thirteen and Jay Hackett got a crew cut? And you told him he looked like a beaver's butt, so he decked you. Old as he was, I think nineteen? I thought that punch was going to split your head right open. But before I could jump in to help, you popped back up, laid him out and his two brothers."

He looked up at Joseph and was sure he would get a response, but none was forthcoming.

Four months later and still there was no improvement. Mr. and Mrs. Connell kept him company on this Saturday night. Billy was at home with Lily and their newborn baby boy. Tests showed Joseph had more brainwave activity, though the medical team still cautioned that the chance of him regaining consciousness was considered improbable in the extreme.

On this lonely evening Mrs. Connell sat near the left side of his bed and read from her Bible, while Mr. Connell sat next to her. His room was dark except for the small reading light on the wall, which Mrs. Connell leaned into, while Mr. Connell was a saddened silhouette in the darkness.

"If the flesh came into being because of the Spirit, it is a wonder. But if the Spirit came into being because of the flesh, it is a wonder of wonders. Indeed, I am amazed at how this great wealth makes its home in this poverty," she recited.

She closed her Bible and leaned back into the darkness. Mr. Connell leaned forward to talk with his boy.

"You've got to come out of this soon, Joey. Winter will be in retreat before we know it and you know as well I do, that as spring makes its way north to us there is an abundance of work to be done around the ranch. I'm not as young as I used to be and nothing would please me more than to be standing beside you, letting you do most of the work for me. Happy misses you terribly. It's the way she whinnies at me. I know it's not me she wants visiting her," he said.

A nurse pushed open the door to Joseph's hospital room to deliver a message.

And as that door slowly opened in the world without, *Joseph continued his battle in his world within.*

With the first attacking warrior knocked to the ground Joseph turned his venom toward the second warrior directly in front of him. The third warrior could have easily cut him in two through the waist, but mysteriously did not. Joseph was too focused on the attacker in front of him to notice this unexplained inaction. He went on the attack with his own overhead sword strike, forcing the second warrior to step back in a defensive posture.

But now... but now, Joseph's unprotected back was an easy target for the third warrior. This adversary flipped his sword from his right hand to his left, curled his powerful hand into a fist, and drove his fist with penetrating fury into Joseph's back, square at the base of his spine. Shockwaves of overwhelming pain shot through his body. His powerful legs buckled and he fell to his knees. He could barely breathe and for a moment no sound could escape his lungs. Blood spewed from his mouth.

All three warriors stood over him, their swords ready but not put to use. Joseph's torso recoiled as he struggled to breathe and recover.

Moments passed.

Still the warriors did not attack.

He regained his breath and anger shoved fear aside with a renewed determination and vigor of purpose. Still on his knees Joseph let out a primal scream and swung his sword at the third warrior. The man retreated a step back out of range.

Joseph rose to one knee as the second warrior now swung his sword down with fury, but his strike was deflected in a loud clash of metal as Joseph counter-attacked and rose to his feet. He loaded up and threw a roundhouse kick with everything he had and caught the man square in the liver, dropping him in his place.

Joseph returned his attention to the first warrior and faked a high attack, then cut low and severed the man's legs at the knees. He turned without pause and lunged at the third warrior and smacked him in the temple with his sword, killing the man instantly.

Now it was one on one. His rage grew with a sense that freedom might be his. He swung his sword at the lone warrior's unprotected neck. The man leaned back. But not far enough, as Joseph's sword cut through his jugular vein. He fell to the ground mortally wounded.

Joseph's chest heaved in the delirium of freedom. But the sensation was short lived. In the dark night of black gloom a statue appeared.

It was of four lions perched atop a pedestal. Each lion, twice the size of any earthly cat, sat with their backs to each other so each faced one of the four directions. Around the outside of the pillar, under each lion, was a carved wheel with twenty-four spokes. Between the first two wheels was the image of an elephant. Between the second and third was a galloping horse. Between the third and fourth was a bull. And finally between the fourth and first was another lion.

Joseph studied the statues for a moment, but a moment was all he had. All four lion statues came to life, leapt off of the pedestal and swarmed him in attack.

Paralyzed with fear he dropped his sword. The lions charged with no regard for the warrior corpses under their paws. Joseph knew death was charging at him with razor sharp fangs ready to tear him to pieces and he was powerless to stop them.

Back in the world without, the nurse who had entered his hospital room whispered, "Mr. Connell, there's a call for you. It's your son, Billy."

Mr. Connell rose and followed her to the phone at the nearby nurse's station.

Joseph's left hand twitched.

Back in his world within, three of the charging lions slowed their speed so one could take the lead. It roared in terrifying purpose and flew through the air at Joseph, knocking him hard to the earth below as it landed atop his chest. Its massive paws draped on either side of his head.

He cried out, "I want to…"

Joseph's mother clasped her Bible when the silence in the room was unexpectedly broken.

"…go home," Joseph whispered.

Mrs. Connell's eyes opened wide. She jumped from her chair, threw open the door to his room, and screamed into the hallway, "John! John! He's awake!"

CHAPTER 5

On a warm spring day the horses grazed in the corral. The grasslands were at their most nutritious and green and that pleased the horses and cattle to no end. Billy stood not far from the fence and caught a football thrown to him. It had some pep to it.

"Hey, not so hard," he playfully complained and threw the ball back.

Joseph caught the football with his left arm. His only usable limb. He sat in his wheelchair and used his emaciated body as a brace for the ball so he could line his fingers up on the laces, get a good grip, and throw it back to Billy.

His legs and right arm were paralyzed and lifeless. He had been back home now going on two months since he miraculously awoke in the hospital. But in the passage of the past year, his right arm and legs had wasted away to little more than skin and bone in appearance. His hair was shorn close and his badly scarred face and scalp had nowhere to hide. Plastic surgery was still in its infancy as a medical specialty, but the surgeons had done an admirable job of reconstructing his face as best they could over many surgeries. Though there were undeniable limits to what they could accomplish. His Hollywood good looks and youthful vigor of body and spirit were long gone.

He came back home a week shy of his nineteenth birthday to the great joy of his parents and brother. They wanted to throw him the biggest welcome home birthday party ever seen in Montana, but Joseph refused. He would not even let anyone acknowledge his birthday, as to him it would forever mark the day he had been crippled. His mother had asked him to not use that word. It sounded so unkind and was not how she saw him. But it was how he saw himself.

Joseph threw the ball back, but too hard and too far, which forced Billy to run and retrieve it. When he turned back around he saw that Joseph had wheeled himself away, closer to the horses inside the corral. Billy walked over to him and could see tears streaming down his face as Joseph looked up at him. Through his tears he told his older brother that he wanted to go back. Back to the time he was a very little boy. Back before the nightmares had come for him like demons.

Billy knelt down. Joseph told him that sometimes, sometimes while he slept, in his dreams he forgot because he was running and playing. But then every morning he woke up and life broke his heart all over again, he sobbed.

Billy leaned in and lovingly told Joseph that he was a miracle. Everyone said so from the doctors to Pastor David. That he was lucky to be alive. That he needed to accept this and live his life. Joseph protested from the depths of despair. He reached into his mouth, ripped out his dentures and threw them to the ground. He mouth curled in around his gums like that of an old man. He cried out and pushed Billy away from him with his one limb that still worked. Billy fell backwards and felt the stinging pain in his jaw.

He got back to his knees as Joseph cried without restraint, took his little brother in his arms, and told him it would be okay. It would be okay. He promised it would be.

If belief was required to tell your little brother something to make him feel better, then Billy was lying. The truth was no one knew if Joseph would ever be okay. Billy was not lying about Joseph being a miracle. The fact that he survived his accident was a miracle. The fact that he woke up even more so. That he suffered no permanent brain damage was medically inexplicable. And that he had even the use of his left arm mystified doctors. That was the feel good news.

But the reality was not so comforting. Joseph had refused to go to work in the bottling plant with his father and brother. Even after Mr. Connell had a contractor install a special elevator that led directly into Joseph's newly constructed office. He did go to see it once out of respect for his father, but responded that it only made him feel like a mole that never left his tunnel and that he was a freak to be pitied. It broke Mr. Connell's heart to hear his boy talk about himself that way.

Joseph was grateful to his father but he could not bring himself to put on a brave face for the hundreds of employees he would see every day. Their genuine kindness only made him feel worse.

Mrs. Connell would often find Joseph sitting naked in front of the mirror in the bathroom in his wheelchair. He seemed to study every inch of his broken body. Every scar that defined his face. Sometimes his gaze was locked on the catheter bag with the tube inserted through his urethra and into his bladder. Sometimes on the colostomy bag whose tube was permanently inserted through his abdomen and into his colon to collect waste matter.

She feared what he was thinking but did not press him. Instead she would enlist his help in her garden. When he would try to refuse she would remind him that he still had one good limb and that he would earn his keep on the ranch. Joseph knew what his mother was doing and he couldn't break her heart any more by refusing her.

When he did leave the house of his own accord Mrs. Connell would watch him in his wheelchair. It had been modified for him so that both wheels turned together. She noticed that he often seemed to want to know just how far he could navigate the ranch. Getting around the house was no problem for him as Mr. Connell had built the house as a single story dwelling with no stairs. Making his way up and down the circular driveway took careful effort on his part, but he could manage it thanks to the meandering path that Mr. Connell had created.

The rest of the property was a challenge. The reality was that he couldn't make it anywhere past the horse corral and barn. About the only time she chose to believe Joseph felt comfort was around the horses, who would approach him one at a time with head lowered so that he could rub each on the nose. Happy was still selfish and greedy with her allotted time.

But otherwise, the natural foothill mountains were too steep to travel for a young man in a wheelchair with the use of one arm only. Mrs. Connell would watch painfully through the window as Joseph would try and fail to make his way further around the ranch. He had nowhere to go anyway. But that too was a source of anguish for him.

What had been the majestic beauty of the horses he loved so dearly and the breathtaking countryside now was determined to torment him. Keeping him a prisoner of the land. The days marched on without relief.

It was on a nondescript afternoon in the middle of the week that Joseph sat looking out the window while listening to the radio. The music hour had ended and the talk radio portion came on. The radio announcer introduced a psychiatrist from India by the name of Dr. Patel. He had come to the United States four years ago to launch the International Metaphysics Society, which he hoped would bridge the gap between the pursuits of Western medicine and Eastern mystical practices.

The strange practices from India of yoga and meditation were becoming more familiar to Westerners as were the alleged abilities of mind over matter that mystical monks in India could use to perform what seemed like magical feats of levitating and not bleeding even when their flesh was pierced.

Dr. Patel was interested in how these seemingly magical techniques could be used to improve and enhance the lives of his patients. He had one patient in particular that he was very excited to tell the radio audience about. The man's name was Kevin and he was a full quadriplegic from birth, which meant that he had spent the first forty years of his life lying flat on his back, as even an assisted attempt to sit in an upright position would cause his blood pressure to drop so severely that he would pass out.

Dr. Patel had wondered if a very simple Eastern practice from India of mindfulness mixed with biofeedback could "teach" Kevin to raise his blood pressure solely with the power of his mind, by turning inward and using his consciousness to direct his blood pressure to rise and stay raised enough to allow him to sit up for extended periods. To the childlike glee of both doctor and patient, it had worked.

Joseph looked over at the radio and listened more intently.

The radio broadcaster asked Dr. Patel if it was true that humans only used ten percent of their brain capacity and was that where this magical power might come from? Dr. Patel laughed and replied that no, that was just an urban legend, though it depended on one's point of view. While it was true that humans used one hundred percent of their brain, that did not necessarily imply that they used one hundred of the brain's capacity. And therein perhaps lay the difference that mystical monks were able to harness, to train their consciousness in chemical form to be more powerful and more self-aware.

Dr. Patel likened it to driving a car at only twenty miles per hour, when with a heavy foot on the gas petal and more gas in the engine, that same car might barrel down the road at sixty, seventy, even eighty miles per hour.

Joseph was now fully paying attention to the broadcast.

The radio announcer mentioned that there was another man in the studio with them and from the way he was dressed it was clear that he was not only a monk from India, but that he was also a practitioner of these mystical practices. He was an old man dressed in a simple brown garment.

Dr. Patel asked the old man to please describe this mind over matter phenomenon. The old man explained that his ancestors would describe it as taking voluntary control over the body. That is to say, making the involuntary the voluntary. Making the unseen, seen. By the mind's eye, which controlled all. Dr. Patel then interjected that as Albert Einstein so beautifully shared with the world in his famous $E=mc^2$ equation, matter and energy are the same thing in different forms. That by turning consciousness inward it just might be possible to experience the root existence of both matter and energy. And that is what is referred to as "cosmic consciousness."

The radio announcer asked the old man to explain what cosmic consciousness was to him personally. His guest, who had kindness etched upon his face, replied that it was an illusion that the energy of our minds and the matter of the universe were two different things. But what was most important... what was most important, the old man said, as he hesitated and leaned into the microphone, was to know that... *each must travel the path laid bare.*

Joseph froze and the hairs on the back of his neck stood up. He had heard that voice before. From the old man who visited him in the locker room. It was the same person on the radio. The rest of the broadcast was a blur.

CHAPTER 6

It took Joseph an hour on the phone, pleading with the secretary, the assistant manager, and finally the general manager of the radio station to have Dr. Patel call him back before he and the old man left the studio. He sat by the phone, barely moving a muscle, barely blinking until the phone finally rang.

Joseph eagerly picked up the receiver and thanked Dr. Patel for calling him back. He asked the doctor if he could please put the old man on the phone. He explained that they had met once before and he would very much like to speak with him again. Dr. Patel said that he was sorry, but the old man had already departed to catch his flight back to India.

Joseph's heart sank.

But he recovered. He asked Dr. Patel if he could teach him to walk with the same biofeedback or mind over matter tricks or whatever else he had taught Kevin to raise his blood pressure. Dr. Patel replied that he wished that he could, but Joseph was asking for a miracle well beyond his capabilities. He explained that the threshold for raising one's blood pressure was akin to a baby crawling. While getting neurotransmitters to jump across nerves that had been severed in the spinal column was like trying to run faster than the speed of sound.

It may seem like a tiny distance to him and medically speaking it was. But to the chemical neurotransmitters the distance between severed nerves was farther apart than the Earth was to Mars.

Joseph would not give up. He asked Dr. Patel if that old man who was with him today could teach him to get up from his wheelchair and walk with the power of the mind. Dr. Patel said that as a man of medicine he would have to say no. However, as a man of faith who had heard of magical legends as a boy that mystical monks of India were allegedly able to perform, he would say that he would not rule it out.

Dr. Patel let Joseph know that the old man had left his address should anyone wish to contact him. But he lived deep up in the Himalayas of India.

Joseph thanked Dr. Patel and wrote down the address for the old man.

Later that night Joseph told his parents about the radio show he had listened to, about the man Kevin who could now sit up, about Dr. Patel, and about the old man in India that he needed to go see. Mr. and Mrs. Connell were initially happy to see Joseph so full of energy and spirit for the first time since his accident. But both quickly shot down his idea. India was some mysterious far off country. He could barely navigate his way around the ranch he had been born on and grew up knowing every blade of grass.

Joseph protested that he needed to go find this man. He desperately needed to go and that he would be fine. Billy would take him. Mrs. Connell asked if Billy had already agreed to this. Joseph admitted that no, he hadn't actually asked him yet, but that he was sure that he would. Mr. Connell fell silent. Mrs. Connell told Joseph that it broke her heart to disappoint him, but that they could not allow him to go. It was too dangerous. It was too uncertain. It was simply not possible.

Joseph had fought. But had been defeated again. He did not speak unkind words. He did not lose his temper. He did retreat further and further into himself. Days passed into weeks and weeks became a month. Then two. And still he could not shake the feeling that he did not belong in Montana. But no one would listen to him.

He sat outside the house one night, watching the sun set as the fire from the fire pit warmed him. Billy pulled up in his pickup truck. Their mother had called him and asked him to sit with Joey. He got out and sat on a rock next to Joseph in his wheelchair.

"Dad's still hoping you'll change your mind and come work at the plant with us," Billy tried to comfort him.

"That God damn deer just wouldn't move," Joseph replied.

Billy stared at him.

"You know how you hear those stories about people waking up from an accident and they don't remember anything? Want to know the last thing I remember? It was the crack of my neck breaking like a twig when my face hit that tree. It was the loudest sound I ever heard. I don't know why some people are cursed," he said.

"Joey, you're not–," Billy started to say, but Joseph cut him off.

"I am."

He took a deep breath and then...

"I hate God, Billy. And I don't care if that damns me to Hell," Joseph said and wiped a tear from his eye.

Billy stood up and walked to his little brother. He leaned down, put his hand around the back of his head, and pulled him in close. Then tenderly kissed his little brother on the forehead.

The very next morning Joseph wheeled himself down from the house to the corral of horses. He was late and knew that Happy would be sure to let him know. As he was about to pass the red barn on his right, he looked over to the custom saddle that his father and brother had commissioned to be made for him. It hung on the wall just inside the left barn door. The saddle he had never ridden. Below it were the beautiful pair of custom boots his mother had hired a gifted bootmaker to craft for him. Every detail of the stitching up the sides was a perfect match for the sketch he had scribbled as a boy.

Joseph couldn't bring himself to put those beautiful boots on legs that didn't work, so he left them where he felt they belonged. Among the horses in the barn. He decided to wheel himself over to feel the soft leather of the saddle and admire the boots again up close.

A few feet from the barn Joseph was suddenly and violently face down on the gravel. It happened so fast he was in shock. It took him several moments to get his bearings and understand what had happened. His wheelchair had caught on a rock and toppled him off to the left. He fell without warning. His reflexes, diminished to his one good limb, had kicked in and he had partially broken his fall with his left hand, which was now bloody from the gravel, while his face was cut and full of dirt.

Joseph looked up and could see the horses in the corral trying to come to his aid. But they could not get out of the pen. He squirmed and managed to brace his left hand on the ground to try to turn himself over. But he couldn't move.

After his accident Mr. Connell had hired two part-time ranch hands to do the chores that needed to be done that Joseph in his coma certainly could not perform. Broken fences needed to be repaired, cattle needed to be guided to rotating grasslands, and the horses needed to be fed the bales of hay. The most efficient way to get such a large quantity of hay into the corral for the horses to eat was load it into the back of the pickup truck, back the pickup truck to the corral, and use the pitchfork to shovel the hay over the fence. Which the two part-time ranch hands had done right on schedule. But one of them had left it on the ground instead of putting it back to hang on the wall where it belonged.

When Joseph fell from his wheelchair, his right leg was impaled on the thick, razor sharp metal teeth of the pitchfork, which was why he couldn't turn himself over.

He couldn't feel anything as the pitchfork penetrated his leg. But as he looked down at his body he could see the teeth of it protruding out the back of his right thigh.

The merciless metal cut through Joseph's atrophied muscle tissue like butter. Two years ago when he was the most fearsome fighter for hundreds of miles his thigh bone would have been a formidable adversary to the pitchfork entering his body. But in its weakened condition it had shattered like glass.

Joseph was not in any physical pain, though his spirit had once again been violated. He reached down, grabbed the pitchfork by the wooden handle just above the metal spikes, and used it as leverage to flip himself onto his back. His bloodstream flooded with adrenaline and he hyperventilated for a moment. Then two. But he calmed himself down. There wasn't much blood to speak of on the ground so he must not have severed his femoral artery or he knew that he would already be dead.

He rested his head back down on the ground, trying to decide what he wanted to do. Perhaps this was a blessing. If he simply pulled the pitchfork out of his thigh he would certainly bleed out. And be done with it. He was sad that he would not get to say goodbye to his family, whom he loved so dearly. As he knew they loved him.

But it was time to go.

Joseph reached down and again grabbed the wooden handle of the pitchfork. He took a deep breath and pulled with all his might. Certain in the knowledge that the end would be nigh and that he could finally rest. But the pitchfork had no intention of complying with his wishes and would not even budge from his flesh, much less leave it completely. For rest was not what awaited him. He tried again and again, but was weaker with each futile effort.

He finally let his weary head crash back down to the gravel and cried. Then screamed for his mother.

Mrs. Connell could never say for sure whether she heard Joseph calling for her or whether she just knew. Without warning the knitting needles flew from her hands as she rose from the couch, ran out the front door and raced down to where Joseph lay impaled on the ground. Mr. Connell followed closely behind. They saw him at the same moment.

She dropped to the ground when they reached him and cradled his head in her lap. He looked up at her, unable to speak, and her heart broke as she wiped the dirt and blood and gravel from his face. Mr. Connell knew that if he pulled the pitchfork out, Joseph would be dead in seconds. So he grabbed the wooden handle just above the metal teeth with both hands.

This pitchfork was no Ponderosa pine. It was hickory. Five times stronger than Ponderosa, which made it just the right wood for the heavy lifting that a pitchfork was used for. Mr. Connell's blood boiled with rage. He grabbed that hickory handle with both hands and snapped it like kindling to throw into a fire. He then picked up his boy, with the metal fork still through his thigh, and carried him to his pickup truck as Mrs. Connell cradled his head.

They drove at a dangerous speed to the hospital twenty miles away. Joseph was unconscious and limp as he lay on his mother's lap. Mrs. Connell, who would not let herself cry the night of Joseph's accident for fear that it would loosen her grip on keeping him here, now could not fight back the tears that fell from her cheeks and mixed with Joseph's blood that stained her handmade dress.

The hospital staff could not believe that Joseph was back again and so gravely wounded. The surgeon explained to Mr. and Mrs. Connell that he was confident that he could save Joseph's life, but the leg would have to come off. It was the most prudent approach, to amputate just below the hip. Mrs. Connell refused and told him that he would not be cutting off her son's leg. The surgeon explained that an amputation would actually be easier and safer than operating on his impaled leg, as well as be less likely to result in sepsis, which was blood poisoning and could lead to death.

Mrs. Connell did not care about his medical training nor his protocol nor his opinion for that matter. Her Joey had survived more than a dozen surgeries and he would warrior through a dozen more if need be. His body was already broken. She would not allow a part of it to be chopped off with a bladed saw not much different than a lumberjack would use to cut down a tree. He would never survive waking up to see his leg gone. She ordered the surgeon to God damn save it.

For she was not sending Joseph off to India to learn to walk again missing a leg.

CHAPTER 7

Joseph did survive the surgery and he did keep his leg. When he woke up in his hospital bed he looked down before even speaking to see if his leg was still there. His mother nodded. Mr. Connell took him by the hand as Billy told him he was taking him to India. It took three months for his leg to heal enough for the surgeon to give his approval that it was safe for him to travel.

On a clear summer day in August Joseph sat in his wheelchair outside the Connell house as Billy pulled his pickup truck up to him. Today these two brothers, neither yet old enough to legally drink alcohol, would be on a nineteen hour fight halfway around the world to a strange land in search of a fantastical elixir that a teenage boy needed to believe could be found. Billy's wife, Lily, stood holding their baby boy, James. Mr. And Mrs. Connell stood next to her. As Billy exited his pickup truck and walked around to open the passenger door, Mr. Connell reached down and scooped Joseph in his arms and carried him over to the front seat.

Billy folded Joseph's wheelchair and placed it in the bed of the pickup truck along with the duffel bag. Mr. Connell stared at his maimed son for a moment. He told his boy that he loved him and always would, then reached into his pocket, took out an orange baseball cap and placed it on Joseph's head.

"Take this. I hear it's damn hot over there. Hotter even than Montana," Mr. Connell said.

Joseph smiled at his father. Mr. Connell looked at his youngest son with a heart full of sad acceptance assuaged by the beauty of sacrifice.

"Joey, when you were a little boy all I wished for you was to be happy. As you got older I prayed only that you would find peace. So if traveling eight thousand miles away from us is what you need to do to find it, then every single mile is worth it," Mr. Connell said.

Joseph smiled as such unconditional love washed over him. "Thanks, Dad," he said through a smile of gratitude.

It was Mrs. Connell's turn to say goodbye. She gave him a tight hug and pressed her cheek to his.

"Being your mother is what I was born for, Joey," she whispered and gave him a kiss.

As Joseph and Billy drove to the airport Lahiri was busy eight thousand miles away making preparations.

He lived high up in the Himalayas in a small one story white house built of stone. This day he had important labors to complete. One by one he carried large rocks that took both hands to hold and a good deal of strength to lift and place each one in the backyard of his house. One after the other he positioned them on the ground no more than one foot apart until a hundred such rocks filled all the space between the back of his house and three tombstones fifty feet away.

The middle tombstone was larger than the two on either side of it. Each had writing inscribed on it in Hindi, the native language of India.

Joseph sat in the window seat of the plane with Billy next to him. It had been a long flight and the brothers had slept for most of it. But now they were soon to touch down in a strange new land and neither knew what to expect. Joseph looked out the window at the gravel covered mountains thousands of feet below. The reflection of the sun's rays made the mountains appear a pale gold broken up by shadows cast from higher ridges above.

The flight attendant spoke over the loudspeaker and announced that in thirty minutes they would be landing in New Delhi, the capital of India. An hour later Billy pushed Joseph in his wheelchair through the airport as they made their way toward the exit. The terminal bustled with people dressed in ways the brothers had never seen before. For while some Indians dressed in Western styles of pants and dress shirts, most were attired in traditional Indian clothing. The women dressed in brightly colored *saris* – a silk or cotton one piece garment that covered the body from the shoulders all the way down to the ankles. The men wore loose fitting cloth pants with a long shirt that flowed down to the knees.

Some of the men wore turbans, which meant that they were members of the Sikh religion, founded in India back in the fifteenth century. Its followers believed in obtaining peace and salvation through positive actions and pursuing their reunion with God.

India was also the birthplace of Buddhism. Its founder, the Buddha, was born a wealthy Hindu prince in 573 BCE in northern India. Yet, he gave up his great wealth to wander the land penniless to learn the cause of human suffering, which he determined was an out of balance attachment to desire in all its endless forms.

The vast majority of Indians were Hindus, followers of Hinduism. It was the world's oldest religion, which dated back five thousand years and encompassed the belief in reincarnation, yoga, karma, mystical insights and one true God who could manifest in millions of different forms.

These two young brothers had indeed entered a most enigmatic country, where Nirvana was believed to exist but only to those who understood how the senses misled and the eyes were incapable of true sight. Joseph was busy drinking in his new surroundings when Billy pushed his wheelchair over to a currency exchange desk to trade in their American dollars for the local currency of Indian *rupees*. Since each dollar was equivalent to five rupees, Billy was handed back a bigger handful of money than he had turned in, plus a handful of silver coins.

He handed one of the coins to Joseph.

"Here, Joey, hold on to this coin. Maybe it will bring you good luck," Billy said.

Joseph took the coin and looked at the heads side first. He noticed that it was impressively ornate, with a big number five in the middle. Above the number was some writing in Hindi and underneath the number was the word *RUPEES* with the year it had been minted, while the edges had decorative floral designs.

He flipped the coin over in his hand to look at the tails side.

Billy stood behind him counting the bills he had been handed. When Joseph saw what was on the tails side of the coin a halting chill swept over him. It was the statue of the four lions, perched atop a cylindrical pillar, who had come to life in his visions and violently attacked him.

The very same lions.

Billy finished counting the money and noticed Joseph staring at the coin, not moving, barely it seemed even breathing.

"Hey, what's up, little brother?" Billy asked.

"Lions," Joseph answered in a low whisper.

"What?" Billy followed up, unable to hear him.

"Lions," Joseph said again, still disoriented.

"Oh, yeah, lions. Well, we put an eagle on our quarter. I'm sure other countries use a bear or a horse, well, maybe not a bear exactly. Anyway, I read about that. Those lions are the official emblem of India," Billy replied.

The more Joseph learned the more rattled he became.

"Emblem of India?" he asked, still in a fog.

"Yeah, something about an ancient emperor, I think. Pretty cool if you ask me."

Joseph was shaken and clasped at the coin with fear. Billy pushed him in his wheelchair outside to the taxi area, where the brothers were struck by the intense heat.

Having grown up in Montana they were not unfamiliar with high temperatures, but this heat was thick and heavy in a way they had never experienced. Hundreds of taxi drivers waited but Billy quickly made eye contact with one whose friendly smile was impossible to miss. The man walked directly up to them.

"Come, my friends, I will take you where you desire," he said as he lifted Joseph's duffel bag and placed it in the trunk of his car.

He spoke with affection, as if he had picked them up a hundred times before. The fact that he had never met them was no impediment to this. The taxi driver was not only exceedingly friendly in tone but body language as well, which was the custom throughout India. He offered the sincerity of friendship as if he had known them for years. As he spoke he tilted his head to the side and gestured with his right hand in a guiding motion. His body language like that of all of his countrymen was soft, fluid, and non-aggressive as if to say, "as you wish," without the need for the words.

Billy was himself a bit overwhelmed and saw no reason to look a gift horse in the mouth. He pushed Joseph's wheelchair up to the rear passenger door and opened it to let Joseph lift himself into the back seat. While the Connell pickup trucks were too high for Joseph to get himself into, this taxi in India was the perfect height for him to do so unassisted. Billy joined him in the back seat and showed the driver a piece of paper with the address they needed to go to. The driver looked it over and smiled. He then looked back at Billy.

"My friend, this address is very far away. Very far away, indeed. You will get there much faster by train. I will take you to the station," he said.

"Thank you," Billy replied gratefully.

Joseph said nothing, still rattled by the sight of the lions on the coin. As the taxi left the airport and merged onto the local highway it felt to the brothers that they had been magically transported into their very own *Wizard of Oz*. The air was pungent. Not polluted, but thick with life. The roadways were an endless sea of humanity and animal life that all moved like raging rapids coursing in every direction all at once.

Cars, large commercial trucks carrying thousands of sun baked bricks, and endless motorcycle riders shared the roads with elephants ridden by their owners, goats driven forward by a man with a stick, bicycle rickshaws, motor scooters, pedestrians, and water buffalo pulling carts loaded with vegetables. Each participant in this endless orchestra of movement clamored for the right of way on the congested asphalt.

All of these travelers moved within inches of each other, yet no one except these two young men from Montana seemed the least bit perturbed by the arrangement. Horns shrieked relentlessly. Not in anger but as a necessary means of communication to avert a million accidents that seemed destined to unfold yet did not. The eardrums of Billy and Joseph were accustomed to the soothing sounds of nature and horses in Montana, not the cacophony of swooping vehicles and animals that all shared these roadways.

Billy and Joseph stared in shock as they passed a family of five all riding on one motorcycle. The father driving it, his toddler daughter seated on the gas tank between his legs, his five-year-old son behind him, but in front of his wife who held a small baby. Not one member of this family hurtling through time and space on the motorcycle wore a helmet nor seemed the least bit concerned about dodging trucks or slow moving animals large and small.

Joseph was anxious and not sure what he had gotten himself into. Billy sought to comfort him.

"We're not in Kansas anymore, Toto," he said.

That lightened Joseph's state of mind.

"Well, if I'm Toto then I suppose you're the Scarecrow," he smiled back.

The roadway leading to the train station was filled with deep potholes, which caused the taxi to bounce up and down over and over again. The driver looked in his rear view mirror to check on his new friends.

"This roadway is called 'Digestion alley.' Very good for the internal organs to process the food stuff. This is my favorite for after a good meal," he said while moving his right hand in a circular motion in front of his stomach.

Minutes later they pulled into the train station.

"Sir, may I again see the address to which you are traveling?" the driver asked.

Billy gladly showed him the piece of paper again.

"Yes, yes," said the driver. "Take this train to Haridwar and from there you can hire another local taxi as far as he will take you into the Himalayas. From there you can hire a farmer to transport you to your address by oxen."

"Oxen?" Billy asked. "Couldn't you just drive us? I'll pay you whatever you want."

"Sir, firstly, as I mentioned, you will get there much faster by train than by taxi. Secondly, a car cannot navigate to this place you seek. There are no roads at the top of the earth. I cannot say for sure if even there are people at this place you are traveling to," he said with a reassuring smile.

"Okay," Billy replied.

"Sir, may I ask you a question?" the driver asked.

"Sure," Billy answered.

"Well, Sir, India is the most beautiful country in the whole world. She has magnificent temples and the greatest expression of love ever witnessed in the Taj Mahal. She produces the world's finest silks and fabrics. There is so much beauty to see and discover," he said.

The taxi driver was not being immodest at his country's impressive creations. At the height of the Roman Empire, India's spices were so highly valued that its pepper was worth more than gold by weight. It was India who gave to the world the invention of six-sided dice for game play and who would one day give rise to computers by inventing the concept of zero.

"Why then do you wish to travel to such a remote place that even most Indians have never been to?" he asked.

Billy looked over at his brother.

"Because I need to find someone," Joseph replied.

"Well then," said the taxi driver, "You will be okay, my friend. Karma has brought you here for a reason and I am sure that it is a most splendid one. Do not be afraid."

The taxi driver then leaned his arm over the seat to be more intimate in conversation and looked Joseph directly in the eyes.

"It looks to me that karma has for you very great plans. Very great plans, indeed," he said.

"Thank you," Joseph replied gratefully.

Hours later the train carrying the brothers continued traveling north through the Himalayas. Joseph and Billy looked out the window and took in the fertile scenery of the Punjabi plains – India's breadbasket of wheat fields that stretched for hundreds of miles.

They sat alone on a bench meant to hold four people. Across from them sat five men packed tightly shoulder to shoulder. Another man walked into the train compartment and sat down on the bench with them. Somehow the five men managed to make room for him.

Billy and Joseph looked at each other, then at the men who sat across from them.

"Please, come sit here next to us," Billy said to the man who had just sat down.

"No, Sir, I cannot. That is quite all right," replied the man.

"But we have plenty of room," insisted Billy.

The man smiled and replied, "We too have plenty of room, Sir. You are a guest in our country. You take all the room you wish. We will no doubt fit another man at the next stop."

"Thank you," Billy replied.

By midnight the brothers were fast asleep on the train as it traveled overnight to their destination. Billy slept on one bench, Joseph on the empty other one across from him. At seven o'clock the next morning the ticket official woke the brothers with a gentle shake.

"Sirs, we have arrived in Haridwar," he said.

The brothers found a local taxicab driver and headed off for the next leg of their journey. Haridwar was one of India's holiest cities, located along the Ganges River at the base of the Himalayas. For centuries upon centuries Indians believed that simply bathing in this sacred river could wash away a person's sins.

The Himalayas were majestic mountains to travel through. Some had no vegetation, some were snowcapped, and some were covered in pine trees. Both brothers were struck not only by the beauty of the mountains but how familiar they felt, as if they could have been mountains they knew back in Montana.

"I didn't expect to see pine trees. I wonder if they're Ponderosa," Joseph asked.

"I don't know, I guess tress are trees," Billy replied.

Joseph burst out laughing, grateful for a moment of levity.

"That's your great insight? 'Trees are trees,'" he said.

Billy smiled and shrugged his shoulders as if to say, "Yeah, that's all I got."

As the trip continued for hours the mountains grew more steep and the turns in the narrow road more tight and hairpin. Billy had the advantage of using his feet pressed against the floor of the taxicab to keep himself from getting jostled from side to side. Joseph had no such ability. He could only grab tightly the handle above the door with his one good limb to keep his maimed body from falling over. It was grueling but he would never complain. He noticed Billy worrying about him.

"I'm okay," he reassured his brother.

Another hour later the taxicab driver stopped and turned around to his passengers.

"I cannot drive you any further. But wait here. I will find a farmer to take you in his oxen cart," he said.

"Thank you," Billy replied.

Joseph was exhausted and let go of the handle over the door and let his dead tired arm drop down to his lap as Billy stepped out of the taxicab to pay the driver and retrieve the wheelchair and duffel bag from the trunk.

Hours later the brothers traveled in the back of an oxen pulled cart. Joseph sat in his wheelchair which was a welcome relief, while Billy sat on the wooden floor. The heat was sweltering. There were no longer any discernible dirt paths. The entire small valley within this mountain range was compartmentalized into mini farms with fields of crops in green, yellow, and red that were so deep and bright they were visually intoxicating.

The brothers saw men and boys work in the fields as women and girls carried the crops in large wicker baskets they held on their heads. Even here, high up in the mountains where families led subsistence lives the women and girls were dressed in brightly colored saris.

Finally, the farmer stopped his cart and pointed off in the distance.

"You will from here have to walk," he said.

Billy looked at Joseph, who nodded that it was okay. So he climbed out of the cart, put Joseph's wheelchair on the ground, and placed him in it. He paid the farmer, then began pushing Joseph in his wheelchair along a long, flat, bare naked stretch of earth as the farmer turned his oxen around and headed back from where he had come. It was still another hour before the brothers could see off in the distance was Lahiri's small one story white house made of stone, situated at the bottom of a rock mountain. As they made their way closer the ground was flat and easy to travel, even for a wheelchair.

Out back Lahiri stood in front of the three tombstones holding a bouquet of flowers. He knelt and placed them in front of the graves.

"I must go now. Dear friends have traveled a great distance to come see us," he said then stood back up.

He turned and made his way back to his house, navigating the obstacle course of large rocks that he had so painstakingly created just two short days ago. He entered the front door and could see Joseph and Billy a mere hundred yards away. Inside the home Lahiri walked to his small kitchen and filled a cloth bag with water from a copper pitcher then placed it on the countertop next to a blue safari hat. He then walked to the front door, opened it, and stood in the doorway as his guests arrived.

Billy pushed Joseph up to Lahiri, who in the silence that hung in the air was given to pause at the emaciated shell of a once vibrant young man who occupied the wheelchair in front of him. Both Joseph and Billy were overheated from their long journey and Billy's hands and wrists ached from pushing Joseph's wheelchair, though he never let on.

Lahiri took the moment to assess Joseph's aura, the flowing energy field that surrounded the human body. It was a form of extra sensory vision acquired through untold years of meditating, sitting still and diving into the unseen world of pure breath until the universe manifested itself from within. Joseph's aura was dim and fractured and in need of healing, just as his body and spirit were.

To a mystic like Lahiri, the physical world witnessed at a deeper level of reality was nothing more than layer upon layer of vibrating energy. He gazed into Joseph's heart where he could see his Spirit trapped on the ground by the lion while the other three formed a menacing circle around him. But a moment later it was time to return his attention to the physical world.

"I see the ice did not work," Lahiri said and smiled.

"Can you help me?" Joseph asked.

"For what are you searching?" Lahiri replied.

"To walk again."

"Why?"

Joseph was flustered. Billy watched on silently.

"So... so I can live my life," he replied.

"Were you living it before?"

Joseph gulped and didn't know what to say.

"Please, may I see your hand?" Lahiri asked him.

Joseph eagerly offered up his left hand and closed his eyes, desperate for his first mystical experience. Lahiri calmly removed Joseph's watch and handed it to Billy.

"He will not be having a need for this," he said.

Billy took the watch as Joseph opened his eyes. Lahiri held Joseph's hand in his hands to soothe him.

"Please, come in," he said to the brothers as he gently let go of Joseph's hand.

He then turned and led the way into his humble home. Both Billy and Joseph were only too happy to get out of the scorching sun. The brothers looked around the inside of the sparsely furnished home. The small center room had an old wooden table with only one chair. To the left was the small kitchen which did not have any running water nor refrigerator.

Lahiri pointed to the small room on the left in the back of the house.

"This is your room, Joseph," he said.

Joseph wheeled himself over to take a look. The doorway had only a purple curtain that was pulled back. He looked in and saw a small wooden desk but no chair and a bed that had a metal bar that ran across the top of the bed, which would make it possible for Joseph to get himself out of his wheelchair and into bed.

Lahiri pointed to the other room.

"That is my bedroom," he said.

He then walked to the kitchen counter and poured two glasses of water from the copper pitcher, then handed them to the brothers, who quickly gulped it down. Lahiri refilled their glasses, put the pitcher back down, then retrieved a wooden stool and placed it near the table.

"Please, Billy, sit and rest," Lahiri said.

Billy was too exhausted to think to ask how Lahiri knew his name. He dropped himself down onto the stool.

"Thank you," he said.

"You are most welcome," Lahiri replied.

"Have you lived here long?" Joseph asked.

"I suppose that depends on what you consider long," Lahiri answered.

Billy looked around the house again and was overcome not by concern but by an overwhelming urge to scoop Joseph up and take him back to Montana, where in his heart he felt he belonged. But he knew that his little brother was drawn to this mysterious place for reasons beyond his comprehension and that whatever forces had pulled him here, it was not for him to decide Joseph's fate.

Lahiri looked at Billy as if reading his mind.

"For your return trip my friend, Mr. Sanjay, will take you," he said.

Lahiri stood and opened the front door. He called off the right side of his house, which was hidden by trees.

"Mr. Sanjay!"

Out from behind the trees came a middle-aged man in a rickety oxen-pulled cart. Billy and Joseph followed to the front door.

"I thought farmers wouldn't come this far?" Billy asked.

"Fill a man's cart full of fresh vegetables and he will come most anywhere," Lahiri smiled.

He walked to the kitchen counter, picked up the bag filled with water and the blue safari hat and handed them both to Billy.

"Please take this for your return trip. The hat will keep the sun's rays from making their home upon your face any further and please drink the water within the hour," Lahiri said.

He then looked Billy in the eyes warmly and said...

"We are all grateful for your efforts new and old."

Billy looked around the otherwise empty small house. He didn't know who "all" referred to, nor what Lahiri meant by "new and old," but he smiled just the same.

He then leaned down and gave Joseph a tight hug.

"Learn this mind over matter stuff quick and come home," he said wistfully.

"I will," Joseph replied with great affection.

Billy then leaned back up and looked at Lahiri.

"Please tell your parents I will keep their son safe," Lahiri reassured him.

"Thank you," Billy replied, then exited the house and climbed into Mr. Sanjay's cart. Joseph watched him get further and further away. He waved one final sad good-bye, then closed the door and wheeled himself back over to Lahiri.

"So, um, how does meditation work?" he asked.

"It frees the mind from illusion," Lahiri replied.

"What kind of illusion?"

"Limitation."

"So then you can get me out of this wheelchair?"

"That is up to you."

"Does, does it take long to learn mind over matter?" Joseph asked.

"Do you have somewhere to go?"

"No."

"You should, it is very hot in India," Lahiri replied with a smile.

Joseph relaxed and smiled back.

"That was a tough fight I saw," Lahiri said.

"Yeah, just my time, I guess."

"Your brother is very kind to bring you so far."

"He's got a wife and baby waiting for him back home."

"Family is important. It is the most important thing."

"Yeah."

"What makes you believe I can teach you to walk again?"

Joseph hesitated a moment, then answered, "Because I need you."

Lahiri smiled.

"You should rest now. You have much work ahead of you."

"I am beat," Joseph replied.

"Come," Lahiri said and led him into his room.

Joseph reached up and grabbed the fortuitous metal bar and pulled himself into bed. He lay down and within moments was fast asleep from exhaustion.

Lahiri walked to him and caressed his forehead for the second time and said...

"Welcome home, Joseph."

CHAPTER 8

Joseph was awakened the following morning by the rising sun. He cleared the cobwebs and lifted himself into his wheelchair using the bar above his bed. As he made his way to the purple cloth draped in his doorway, he stopped and turned his wheelchair around to look back at his bed.

His gaze started at the vertical bar near his pillow, worked its way across the top of the bed horizontally, and finally he looked at the second vertical bar at the end of his bed. He stared at it, wondering how fortuitous it was that the bed had the extra frame necessary for him. After a moment, he wheeled himself out into the main room of the house where Lahiri sat at the table with breakfast ready – a brown lentil dish, whole wheat cirlces of thin bread called *rotis*, and a bowl of homemade yogurt. Also on the table was a pitcher of water.

"Good morning," Lahiri said, while gesturing toward the food. "Please, eat, eat."

Joseph was famished and didn't have to be told twice. He watched Lahiri scoop the lentils onto a *roti* and use it as an edible plate. Lahiri was enjoying the food, so Joseph couldn't wait to dig in.

He copied Lahiri but as soon as he bit into the food his mouth was on fire from the hot spices. He reached past the pitcher of water for the bowl of yogurt and gulped down the entire bowl.

"God damn, that's hot!" Joseph protested.

"How did you know the yogurt would cool your mouth faster than the water?" Lahiri asked.

"I don't know," Joseph replied.

"I see," Lahiri commented.

Joseph noticed a snake crawling on the wooden floor near their feet under the table. He reached down with his left hand and grabbed it, just as he had done countless times back home in Montana, by the back of its head so it couldn't use its fangs to inflict a painful bite.

"Jesus! There's a snake in here," he howled.

"Please, Joseph, do not be so rude."

Lahiri walked over to him and took the snake from his hands. He then turned the head of the snake toward himself.

"Do not be angry with Joseph. He is not housebroken yet," Lahiri said to the snake.

"Me?" Joseph exclaimed. "I save you from getting bitten by a snake, possibly a poisonous one, and I'm the one who's not housebroken?"

"Bitten? By my friend? Do not be so ridiculous. Never. He came looking for food, which in this case happens to be unwanted rodent intruders who will try to eat our crops before we have a chance to pick them," Lahiri replied.

He gently placed the snake back on the floor where Joseph had found it and watched it slither away.

"Well," Joseph protested. "You could at least be impressed that I managed to catch it."

"I will be impressed when you catch it with your right hand," Lahiri said and smiled.

Joseph smiled back.

With the breakfast excitement over, Lahiri walked over to his devotion table nestled between the front door and the kitchen area. On the table were necklace garlands of beautiful flowers, lying in front of a two-foot-high statue in a seated position. It had the body of a human, with four arms instead of two, and the head of an elephant. Lahiri placed the garlands of flowers around the elephant-headed statue's neck. Joseph wheeled himself over and watched.

"What are you doing?" he asked.

"This is Lord Ganesha, the Remover of Obstacles. I am performing a *puga*. It is a daily offering of devotion," Lahiri answered.

"It looks like an elephant head on a person's body. You're offering flowers to an elephant God?"

"That is correct, Joseph. Hinduism has millions of gods, all representations of the One True God. Each of the gods has a purpose. I do this every day."

"The Remover of Obstacles? So you think giving flowers to an elephant-headed God is going to help remove obstacles?"

"It cannot hurt," Lahiri replied.

"Why does he have four arms?"

"So he can remove obstacles twice as fast."

Lahiri walked outside and Joseph followed in his wheelchair, but as soon as he made his way through the door the hot Indian sun hit his badly sunburned skin from his travels the day before. He frantically wheeled himself back to the safety of the inside of the house.

"Holy crap, it's an oven out there!" Joseph said.

He looked down at the sunburned skin on his arms and felt the redness on his face. Lahiri walked back into the house holding long green stalks from a plant he had just picked. Inside them was fresh, jelly-like aloe vera. Lahiri pulled back the green outer layer and rubbed the aloe vera onto Joseph's skin to soothe the sunburn.

"Wow, this stuff feels tingly and I can feel it cooling my skin down. But it smells like something that should have been thrown out six months ago."

"That is the plant's way of making sure you appreciate the sacrifice it has made for you."

"Thank you."

"Do not thank me. I am not the one cooling you off," Lahiri replied.

"So, you want me to thank a plant?" Joseph asked.

"Did the plant not relieve the pain of your sunburn?"

"Yeah, but it's just a plant."

"I see," Lahiri responded.

He pointed to a wooden basket over in the corner.

"If you would like to bring a small towel to cover your neck, you may find one in the basket over there."

Joseph wheeled himself over to the corner but reached into another basket by mistake, next to the one Lahiri had pointed to. He opened the lid and looked inside, his attention suddenly caught by what he saw.

He reached in and removed a dagger. It was intricate in design, with a foot long metal double edged blade of silver that had a patina sheen to it from age. The beautiful handle was made of ivory and had handcrafted rings carved into it. The end of the handle was capped by a bronze tip, also with painstaking carvings etched into it.

Joseph held it up in the air and admired the impressive craftsmanship and beauty, though he was surprised to find a monk in possession of such a deadly weapon. He turned around in his wheelchair and looked over at Lahiri.

"Um, any special reason you have this beautiful and sharp dagger?" he asked.

"Mosquitos," replied Lahiri.

"Mosquitos?" Joseph asked.

"Mosquitos," again answered Lahiri, who then walked over and took it from Joseph's hand and placed it back in the wooden basket. He then reached into the other wooden basket, retrieved a cloth, and handed it to him.

"It looks very old," Joseph said.

"It is. Very old indeed," Lahiri replied.

An hour later Lahiri was down on his hands and knees working in his garden beside his house, weeding around some plants while pulling out others that were ripe. Joseph sat fidgeting with really nothing to do.

"Could we get started, please?" he asked.

"We have. Today is Thursday. It is gardening day," Lahiri replied.

"I mean, could you start teaching me the mind over matter stuff?"

"Oh, you mean, could I teach you to transform your physical essence into a higher vibrational bliss in tune with the infinite universe?"

"Yes, yes, that is exactly what I mean," Joseph replied, oblivious to the sarcasm.

Lahiri stood up from his gardening duties and brushed the dirt from his garment.

"Well, then. Let us proceed."

He pushed Joseph in his wheelchair several hundred yards away to a flat open area of lush vegetation and gave him the necessary instructions.

"Breathe, Joseph. Sit with your eyes closed. Take a deep breath, hold it for a few moments, and then take an even deeper breath. Hold it for as long as you comfortably can, then exhale. Feel the *prana* fill your body and connect you with the cosmos," Lahiri instructed him.

"What is *prana*?" Joseph asked.

"*Prana* is the life force of the universe. It is in everything you can see as well as everything you cannot. It is what makes the heat from the sun, the grass green, and a rock hard to the touch."

"That's it? Just sit here and breathe?"

"Not exactly," Lahiri responded. "You must be very careful not to move."

"Because it will disturb my *prana* and prevent me from experiencing mind over matter?"

"It is more like mind over death, really. If you move in this field, it is possible you may attract highly poisonous insects flying around this area and there is no antidote that I am aware of. Over many centuries countless would be devotees who could not sit still have met an untimely death in this exact spot."

"But nothing moves but my left arm anyway."

"Then blame your left arm if you are stung and killed."

Lahiri turned and walked back toward his garden to finish his duties.

Over the next several days Joseph spent every waking moment he could following Lahiri's instructions so that he might experience the magical mind over matter phenomenon, yet nothing. It was late in the afternoon on his fifth day in India when he inhaled the largest breath he could force his lungs to accommodate, but still there was no change. He exhaled deeply, gave up, and began to cry. Off in the distance, Lahiri watched him. There was in fact much more that he wished to share with Joseph, but it was not time… yet.

A week later Joseph sat in his wheelchair with Lahiri next to him on a small embankment by the river. Night had just fallen and across the river Joseph could see a small temple and some kind of religious service going on.

Dozens of people had gathered for the event. The only light provided was from the partial moon out that night and fifty candles placed around a young teenage boy, as he sat directly in front of the local Hindu priest. To the boy's left was his mother and to his right was his father. The boy and his father, both dressed in white, were draped together under a white cloth. Joseph could see the priest looking at the boy's father as he imparted instructions.

"What's going on?" Joseph asked.

"This is *Punal*," Lahiri replied.

"What's *Punal*?"

"It is the ceremony to celebrate the boy's passage from his life as a boy into that of a man. He has completed the first phase of life and is now being prepared to enter his second stage."

"Why are they sitting like that?" Joseph asked.

"The father is passing on the wisdom every man must possess. But it is only to be spoken from father to son, and only this once. When the father is done, the priest will ask the boy many questions to determine whether he is ready to be recognized by their community as a man," Lahiri explained.

"What if the boy's answers are wrong?"

"Oh, the father would not permit that to happen."

"How many stages of life are there?"

"There are four. After adulthood comes seclusion to contemplate life and finally a man may return to society to be of service to others, if he wishes."

"How long do the stages last?" Joseph asked.

"Well, that depends on the person. It is not so very different from the West. It could be compared to your thirteenth birthday of confirmation, your twenty-first birthday of drunkenness, marriage, and finally your mid-life crisis by twenty-five," Lahiri said with a grin.

Joseph smiled back and Lahiri jumped at the opening he had worked so hard to create.

"Do you think about God much, Joseph?" Lahiri inquired.

Joseph's smile evaporated and a reflexive scowl came across his face at the mention of that topic.

"No," he replied.

"You do not wonder if He has a white beard and a thick wool robe to match?" Lahiri asked.

"No."

"Do you believe in God?"

"Would it make a difference?" Joseph snapped back.

He respectfully lowered his tone, partly in deference to Lahiri and partly so that he did not disturb the ceremony taking place across the river embankment.

"I just don't like Him very much," he said.

"And why have you judged God so harshly?"

Joseph tried to keep a lid on his anger, but it boiled over again.

"Because He's all powerful, right? Mr. God damned omnipotent! So why does He make us suffer? For his amusement?!" he venomously replied.

Lahiri was unruffled.

"God does not punish, Joseph. God teaches," he calmly replied.

Joseph collected himself.

"Well, he can keep his God damned lessons. I've had all the teaching I can take. And what about, what about innocent people like me? Like, like when someone hurts another person who didn't do anything wrong?" he asked.

"That is most certainly not God. One person hurting another is like a hand curling into a fist to smash the foot," Lahiri replied.

"It's still not fair! Why, why, why is it so easy for some and so hard for others?" Joseph demanded.

"Life is never easy. Not for anyone. We all have our battles to fight."

"But it's still not fair. God had no right to make me a cripple."

"The ancients believed that the universe did not exist for a man until he opened his eyes and created it," Lahiri answered.

"So I created a cripple?" a confused Joseph asked.

"Your soul is trying to tell you it wants to go Home," Lahiri replied.

An hour later as Joseph slept Lahiri sat meditating on a nearby mountain top. His eyes closed, feet crossed in lotus posture, he breathed deeply for a good deal more than air. For his breaths, after so many decades of effort, called forth energy hidden to the naked eye.

Energy in the space around him and energy that was released from within from the seven *chakras* along the human spinal column.

Each chakra was a spinning wheel of light of a different color and energy wavelength. The lowest down at the base of the spine known as the root *chakr*a was red and connected a person to the earth. The highest was the crown *chakra,* purple in color at the top of the head, which connected an advanced adept such as Lahiri to the infinite universe. In between them was the sacral *chakra* which was orange in color at the lower abdomen, then the solar plexus *chakra* which was yellow, then the heart *chakra* which was green, the throat *chakra* which was blue, and finally the third eye *chakra* deep within the brain which was indigo in color.

Each one of these *chakra* energy centers, hidden and dormant to all not initiated in the deeper layers of reality, was the bridge between the material flesh of the body and the spirit world. A world of love always waiting, always hoping, always aching to be reached.

The longer and deeper Lahiri breathed the brighter each *chakra* grew, and so as he summoned breath not capable by an average mortal, his aura grew a brighter and brighter purple energy from his crown chakra that enveloped him.

All powered by his advanced breathing technique that had taken painstaking decades of dedication and sacrifice to achieve.

Great, great sacrifice. With no one to help him. Until Joseph.

The next day Lahiri walked through a meadow not too far from the field where Joseph spent most of his waking hours meditating, without much progress. Villagers used this meadow as a park to have a leisurely lunch. Children of all ages played games, ranging from the simple game

of tag to the game universally played throughout India
– cricket.

Even more than soccer, cricket was played by the rich
and the poor. The rich might have had fancy sporting
equipment, but the poor could enjoy the national obses-
sion just as well with a ball, a handmade wooden stick,
and enough open area to smack the ball far and wide.

As Lahiri walked he carried an American football,
which was a sport unknown throughout India. He may
very well have been the only Hindu in India carrying an
American football. His plan was not to play, but to set in
motion a play of his own.

He continued walking until he came across Vijay, a
slender boy of eight years old, wandering through the
meadow by himself. His older sister, Madhu, age eighteen,
had given him a break from shepherding the family's
cattle with her. She had brought them to a nearby field
to graze on the native grass and told him to go enjoy
himself, since there was not anything that needed to be
done until the animals finished grazing anyway. Vijay
was about to walk over to some boys playing when Lahiri
intercepted him.

He showed Vijay the football and explained to him
that it was a very popular game in America, and showed
him how to throw and catch the ball. Vijay, like any little
boy his age, was naturally curious and eager to play with
a new toy in the form of a football.

As Vijay tossed the ball gently in the air, Lahiri walked
a short distance to three ten-year-old boys playing a game
of tag. He greeted the boys warmly and he told them he

had a job for them. He told them that it was really more of a joke. He pointed over to Vijay playing with the football and told them that in a few days he wanted them to take the football away from him and wrestle him to the ground. None of the boys would agree to do it.

Lahiri took several *rupee* coins from his garment and offered to pay them ten *rupees*. They may have been young boys, but they knew how to strike a better deal. They demanded double and for each of them.

Lahiri relented but said they would get half the money up front and half afterwards. He warned them though that if they hurt Vijay they did not get the rest of their money. The boys told him they understood and the plan was set.

Later that night Lahiri sat on the floor of his white stone house while working on his simple wooden handloom. It had a spinning circle in the center which enabled him to spin the cotton into usable fabric.

Joseph sat in his wheelchair and watched.

"Have you always spun your own clothes?" he asked.

"Not just me, Joseph, but millions of Indians for over a thousand years have spun some of the world's finest fabrics. India has always been a country of riches and not just her fabrics but her spices and raw materials. Such blessed wealth is what motivated many peoples, the Dutch, the French, the Portuguese, and many others to invade her over the centuries. But it was the British who conquered Mother India in 1757 and ruled her for nearly two centuries. Until she gained her freedom and independence very recently in 1947," Lahiri explained.

"I guess that explains why so many people in India speak English," Joseph replied.

"Yes, it does. The British brought a great many technological improvements that benefited India, including a modern system of law, thousands of miles of railroad tracks to transport materials and people, the postal service, the telegraph, and many more," Lahiri told him.

"Wow, then I guess India must be pretty grateful."

"The British also brought starvation, famine, and suffering to millions of Indians by taxing them on their crops and earnings, and forcing them to buy imported British goods and fabrics. Some weavers, who made their living on a handloom just like this one, had their thumbs cut off by British soldiers so that Indians would *need* to pay for the fabrics imported from England," Lahiri said.

"Oh," replied Joseph, unaware of such things.

"Yes, less than twenty-five thousand British soldiers managed to rule over millions of Indians, as incredible as it sounds."

"I didn't know that. Did anyone in your family have their thumbs cut off?"

Lahiri stopped spinning on his handloom and looked Joseph in the eyes.

"No, Joseph. No one in my family had their thumbs cut off," he said.

"Well, I'm glad to hear that," Joseph replied.

"The British soldiers who gave the orders to mutilate had good reasons or so they believed. They did not consider themselves bad people. In fact, they considered themselves good people doing the right thing, who were simply acting for the 'greater good.' The problem is, we are all the 'greater good.'"

Joseph didn't know what to say, so Lahiri decided to lighten the mood.

"India has indeed always been a magical place. In her five-thousand-year history she has never attacked another country, though many others have sought out her shores."

"I am amazed at how some people with so little can be so friendly," Joseph replied.

"A person needs money or material possessions to be friendly?" Lahiri playfully asked.

"That's not what I meant."

"The people of India, whether the richest of the rich or the poorest of the poor, know that it is not what you have that matters, it is what you do in life. It is called *Dharma*."

"What is *Dharma*?" Joseph asked.

"*Dharma* is what you are required to do if you are to advance spiritually. It is the work you must complete. It is your duty in life."

Lahiri had Joseph's curiosity piqued.

"What's my *Dharma*?" he asked.

"That is for you to discover. I cannot tell it to you."

"Oh," a disappointed Joseph said, but then asked, "What's your *Dharma*?"

"You are," Lahiri replied.

He then continued...

"That is why I saved your life in the woods the night you hit the deer."

Joseph was stunned at the news.

"You were there?" he whispered.

"I was."

"And you're the one who called for an ambulance," Joseph said.

"Yes, that was me."

"Why were you there?"

"Because I knew what was going to happen," Lahiri said softly.

Joseph was shocked and deeply hurt.

"But if you knew what was going to happen, you could have prevented me from being stuck in this wheelchair. Why didn't you do something before that deer broke my neck?" Joseph asked, his voice cracking with pain.

"Would you have felt any better if the deer had fulfilled its *Dharma* the next day? Or the day after that? There are some things that cannot be stopped, once they have been set in motion, Joseph. No matter how much we wish they could. I tried to stop the deer that night from the locker room, but you turned me away," Lahiri replied.

Joseph was disoriented by the revelation and couldn't talk about this anymore. He wheeled himself away from Lahiri and toward his bedroom. When he reached the curtain hanging in his doorway, he stopped and looked back.

"Thank you… for saving my life," he whispered, then wheeled himself into his bedroom before he could hear the reply.

"I had to," Lahiri whispered back. "I need you to save mine."

CHAPTER 9

In a dream, an able-bodied Joseph laughed and ran after two small blond boys, ages five and two years old, as they ran up a small grass covered hill in Montana. He caught up to them and tickled them both from behind, causing squeals of laughter and mock protest.

"No tickling, Daddy," the older boy said.

The two-year-old boy, a pudgy little bundle of joy still in diapers, waddled out of sight over the hilltop. Joseph rubbed the older boy's belly as he tackled him and continued the tickling despite the prior protest. After another moment he stood up to go after his younger son.

As he made his way over the hilltop he saw his little boy on the ground in a pool of his own blood – his throat gruesomely slashed from ear to ear. From behind him, Joseph heard his older boy cry out to him.

"Daddy!" the boy yelled.

A startled Joseph turned around, only to find his older son now also on the ground, dead, in a pool of his own blood, his throat slashed the same as his little brother's. A final knife to his psyche arrived in the form of a woman's scream, coming from near his dead two-year-old son.

Joseph turned back around to see his wife lying dead next to their son, her throat as slashed as their two little boys.

An hour after waking from his nightmare Joseph sat in his wheelchair silently by the riverbed and watched the rapids guide the water downstream. The current was strong and would have no problem carrying him. How far he did not know, nor care.

With robotic precision he reached with his left hand into the frame of his wheelchair and one by one took out the parts of the small Derringer gun. He laid each piece on his lap as he stared at the water, assembling the gun without the need to look at the individual pieces.

Joseph had come to India brimming with hope born of desperate need, but also with doubt produced by a tired spirit. Doubt in the form of a small handgun he knew could be easily cloaked within the hollow recesses of his wheelchair.

He couldn't understand his latest torment. He didn't have a wife. He didn't have two little boys. But in the nightmare he felt the overwhelming pain as if they had been real people. He couldn't explain it. And he couldn't take it anymore.

Nearby, Lahiri watched.

Joseph turned his wheelchair so that his right side was close to the water's edge. He knew that even this small one bullet gun, shot at close range, would have enough force to send his toppled body and defeated spirit into the river. Even if the bullet didn't kill him immediately, surely he would drown without much delay.

He picked up the gun and pointed it at his left temple.

Still Lahiri did not move.

Joseph's hand trembled. He did not know what awaited him, if anything, on the other side, but it had to be better than what was constantly lying in wait for him on this side.

He slowly contracted the tiny muscles of his left index finger and pulled the trigger, desperate to stop the madness he could no longer endure.

The trip hammer pulled back until it had reached its loading tension, then fired forward. A shiver seized him as he expected the end to blow a hole clean through his brain, but there was no blast.

He shivered again involuntarily and began to hyperventilate, wondering what had gone wrong. As he stared at the gun that had fired, yet fired no bullet, Lahiri walked up to him quietly.

Joseph pulled his confused gaze away from the gun and up to Lahiri.

"It will not work, Joseph. I know. You cannot go around. You must go through," Lahiri said sadly.

He then reached into his simple brown garment and pulled out a bullet. The one he had secretly removed from Joseph's wheelchair gun while he slept. He stared at the bullet a moment, then silently handed it to a bewildered Joseph, who was still staring at the bullet as Lahiri turned and walked away back toward their house.

Hours later Lahiri sat alone at the table in his house and waited. Dinner sat in front of him, untouched. He wondered in painful rumination if his final act toward Joseph would, in fact, be his final act. Even hours of deep meditation could not replenish his depleted spirit.

What would he say to Joseph's mother and father, who had entrusted their son to him, if he had made the wrong decision in giving him back the bullet?

Finally, Joseph wheeled himself quietly into the house and up to the table for dinner. He used the spoon to pour lentils onto a *roti*. Lahiri followed his lead and ate dinner, choosing first to add some vegetables to his own plate. A moment later Joseph reached down into his lap, picked up the bullet, and placed it on the table. Lahiri said nothing as he reached for the bullet and, with a lightened heart, placed it back into his garment.

Later that evening Lahiri sat on the floor, again spinning cotton on his wooden handloom. Joseph sat reading from a book he had found in Lahiri's house. He flipped the page he had just finished reading and found a coin in the book. He picked it up and stared at the tails side, looking at the date printed on it: 1859.

"Where did you get this penny?" Joseph asked.

"It is a shilling," Lahiri replied.

"Oh."

"A man gave it to me once."

"He must have had it for a very long time."

"Not really," Lahiri said as Joseph examined the coin.

"I was not sure your brother was going to leave you," he continued.

He watched Joseph put the coin back onto the page that he had found it on, close the book, and put it down on the small wooden table next to his wheelchair.

"Billy never liked to leave me anywhere, not even at home. One summer he went to this sleepaway camp up in northern Montana and wanted me to go with him. I wanted to go too. Problem was I was only eleven and Mom didn't want to let me go. It took him four days of convincing but he finally got her to agree."

"Did you have a good time?"

Joseph was momentarily lost in pleasant thought.

"I met Hollie. First time she looked at me, I swear I didn't breathe for a whole minute."

Lahiri raised his eyebrows to acknowledge such an impressive feat.

"Hey, for some of us that's still a long time to go without breathing. Anyway, I won spaz of the week because of her. If we were apart for too long, I sort of got disoriented and just wandered around until I found her. One night Billy made himself scarce and she came over to our cabin. I was so scared. Every time I tried to kiss her, I got lightheaded."

Lahiri smiled.

"What happened?" he asked.

"We kind of dated for the summer. But then... the visions came back. I haven't seen her since."

Lahiri's smile faded as a moment of silence dragged into two, then three. Joseph didn't want to think about that anymore.

"So, how did you, um, become a yogi?" he asked.

"The correct term is *sadhu*, or sage, depending on whom you ask."

"My apologies. So, how did you become a *sadhu*, or sage, depending on whom you ask?"

"Well, it is not exactly a profession."

"I know, but I mean, was it 'predetermined by God' or something?"

"Not everything in life is predetermined, Joseph. Not even by God. I once looked forward to sitting under the white cloth with my son as he would someday grow from a boy into man. You have to be careful. What you whisper has to be loud enough for him to hear but not so loud that anyone else, including the priest can hear you, or he will ask your son impossibly difficult questions."

"Where is your family now?" Joseph asked.

"They were killed, in an accident," Lahiri replied.

"What kind of accident?"

"An unfortunate one."

Joseph didn't know what to say.

"Why did you start karate, Joseph?"

"Because I thought it might help me escape... the visions."

"You should not give up meditating."

"But when I do I can't feel anything," Joseph answered.

"You will," Lahiri replied.

Several days later Lahiri arose especially early so that he could make sure he had a sufficient amount of brightly colored magenta powder, which he now held in his fists down by his sides.

Joseph pushed his wheelchair out of his room to see what was for breakfast that day. When he passed through the curtain in his doorway Lahiri threw the magenta powder all over him. Joseph was unprepared to be enveloped in a thick cloud of mischief. He coughed several times but the vegetable powder was harmless to his lungs.

"Happy *Holi*!" Lahiri exclaimed with the exuberant glee of a small child.

Joseph finished coughing, then asked, "What the hell is Happy *Holi*?"

"Well, it is not Happy *Holi*. It is just called *Holi*. I added the happy part. But to answer your question, *Holi* is the spring festival celebrating the rebirth of life as the seasons change and the death of *Holika*, an ogre goddess who devoured children," Lahiri said.

"So, where's my powder?" Joseph asked suspiciously.

"You are wearing it. But there is more in town. If we leave now we can still enjoy the parade."

Joseph looked down at his magenta covered body and wheelchair, nearly speechless.

"Holy cow. I swear this country finds something to celebrate every God damned day," he finally replied.

"And… this is a bad thing?" Lahiri asked.

It took an hour for them to reach the festival in town but it was well worth the trip. As they reached the outskirts they passed an assortment of street performers, snake charmers, monkey trainers, and *fakirs* – men who seemed to be performing feats of mind over matter, such as piercing their skin with needles but not bleeding.

As Lahiri pushed Joseph past these performers, Joseph noticed one extremely interesting *fakir*, an old man who levitated above the earth. He was draped in a white cloth and he held out in front of him a wooden cane, also draped in the white cloth.

It was obvious that he was levitating because there was clearly nothing visible underneath him that could be holding him up. The meditating *fakir* was in a complete state of quiet bliss as he hovered above the earth below.

Joseph was impressed.

"Wow. Maybe he could teach you some mind over matter tricks and then you would have something useful to teach me," Joseph playfully jabbed.

Lahiri looked over at the attention grabbing fellow.

"He is called a *fakir* and things are not always what they appear to be," he replied.

"Maybe not," Joseph said. "But so far that man has shown me more supernatural power than you have."

"Really?"

"Mmm hmmm."

Lahiri stopped pushing the powdered covered Joseph in his powdered covered wheelchair and walked over to the *fakir*. Who, of course, ignored him because he was in deep cosmic supernatural meditation, though he did manage to jiggle his silver cup seeking a donation.

Lahiri looked back at Joseph, who gave him a "What are you going to do?" look.

That was all the go ahead Lahiri needed. He gently shoved the man, as gently as a shove can be anyway. The levitating *fakir* immediately fell over on his side to the dirt below, knocking the pretty white cloth off of him and his "magical" cane. As he rolled onto the ground, furious, the source of his alleged supernatural power became clear. The weighted cane he was holding was attached to a weighted horizontal piece of wood, which was then attached to the seat the *fakir* was comfortably sitting on, all of which was concealed by the serene white cloth.

It was an impressive feat of balance, to be able to hold himself up with just the heavily weighted cane for counterbalance support. But it was not levitating and it was not supernatural.

Joseph burst out laughing as the furious charlatan yelled at Lahiri in his native language. He swung his hands wildly, collected his wooden contraption and now not so white cloth and headed for another part of town to set up shop again where travelers may not have witnessed this unplanned revelation.

Lahiri walked back over to Joseph and returned to pushing his wheelchair closer to the parade going on in town.

"*Fakirs* have impressive balance, but I do not like *fakirs*. They give us sages a bad reputation as fakers," Lahiri said.

Joseph looked back at Lahiri, smiled at him, then turned his attention to the festival taking place ahead. As they joined the parade area it became a large, moving cloud of brightly colored powder. Magenta was the dominant color of *Holi*, but the air was also filled with clouds of red, green, and yellow vegetable powders. Adults and children took part in the fun as brightly colored papier-mâché costumes of local deities were paraded down the road.

Joseph saw a wooden table with piles of colored powder just waiting to be picked up and thrown, so he wheeled himself over to the table, grabbed what he could, and threw it on as many people as possible. They of course did the same to him. The only thing more impressive than the clouds of flying powder was the laughter that everyone, from the smallest girl to the largest man, enjoyed as they celebrated the *Holi* spring festival.

Days later Lahiri knelt in front of the three tombstones and placed flowers on the ground next to them. Twenty yards away Joseph sat in his wheelchair, unable to navigate the ground covered in the rocks that Lahiri had placed there just before his arrival. Lahiri stood back up and walked over to him.

"Sorry I can't join you," Joseph said.

Lahiri smiled warmly.

"You will. When you can walk to them. My family will wait. Take today off, Joseph. You have earned it."

An hour later Joseph pushed himself in his wheelchair toward the meadow that Lahiri had seen Vijay playing in when he had given him the football. As he got closer he saw the three ten-year-old boys that Lahiri had paid money to on the ground, and underneath them was Vijay, being taunted and slapped. Though not terribly hard, it was no more fun than it was fair.

"Come on, give us the ball," the biggest of the boys said to Vijay, who was about as imposing as a leaf, but managing to not lose his prized possession.

Lahiri had given the three ten-year-old boys explicit instructions to not actually hurt Vijay.

Nevertheless, Joseph was upset by what he saw.

"Hey, get the hell off of him!" he yelled.

He quickly wheeled himself over to the boys and using his one good limb, threw them one at a time off of the dirt-covered Vijay, who still impressively clutched his football to his chest.

The boys had been coached by Lahiri to not do anything to Joseph either, so they simply ran away without saying another word. Mostly, they were too interested in collecting the rest of their loot. Lahiri was within sight of the incident, but behind several trees so he would not be noticed. He would go find his second rate hooligans later and pay them the rest of their money.

Vijay stood up and dusted himself off.

"Are you okay?" Joseph asked.

"I will be fine."

"What's your name?"

"Vijay," the little boy replied.

"My name is Joseph. Is V.J. short for something, like Victor James?"

"Vijay is not my initials. It is spelled V-I-J-A-Y."

"Okay, Vijay. Why were those boys picking on you?"

"I do not know. They have never done so before."

"Well, if you want I can teach you to fight so they can't pick on you anymore," Joseph offered.

"You? You cannot even walk. What can you teach me?" Vijay asked incredulously.

Joseph snorted.

"What can I teach you, huh?" he said.

"Yes, what can you teach me?"

Joseph looked around until he saw just the right size piece of broken concrete by the side of the road, then pointed at it.

"Tell you what, little man, go grab that piece of broken concrete over there and I'll show you."

"I do not understand why I should be picking up a piece of broken concrete," Vijay said back.

"Just go pick it up and I'll show you," a flummoxed Joseph said.

"Okay, but it makes no sense to me," Vijay replied, as much to himself as to Joseph.

He did as he was told, then walked back to Joseph and tried to hand him the broken piece of concrete.

"Here you go," Vijay offered.

"No, you hold it."

"Okay, but what am I supposed to do with it?"

"Just hold it out in front of you," Joseph instructed.

Vijay did as he was told.

"Now, hold it there and don't let it move," Joseph said.

He then took the deepest breath he could muster, curled his left hand into a tight fist, and smashed it into that broken concrete with all the rage and frustration and heartache that still tormented him from within.

The concrete broke into pieces and fell from Vijay's stunned little hands. He looked down at the now smaller pieces of broken concrete as if he had just seen the most impressive magic trick of his life.

Joseph was a bit startled himself by his own feat. He clenched and unclenched his fist to make sure nothing was broken. Except for a fairly good-sized trickle of blood coming from his knuckles where just a moment ago there was skin, he was fine.

He smiled and took a deep breath, then looked up at a very impressed little Indian boy.

"Can you teach me to do that?" Vijay asked.

"Well, no, I can't. But I could teach you to fight in case those boys bother you again," Joseph answered.

"No, that is okay. They have never done so before and I do not think they should be having any need to do it again."

"Suit yourself."

Vijay picked up the football.

"Do you know how to throw that thing?" Joseph asked.

"Not really," Vijay replied.

"Here, give it to me. My brother showed me when I was your age. You want to line your fingers up on the laces and then pull your hand back by your ear, then let the ball roll off your hand as you come forward," Joseph instructed while demonstrating.

A pleased Lahiri looked on and smiled, then walked back toward his home.

The next day Joseph sat meditating in the meadow when he was unexpectedly approached by Madhu, Vijay's eighteen-year-old sister. She was slender and beautiful, standing five feet, four inches tall, with long dark hair, big brown eyes, and a bright infectious smile. She wore a turquoise *sari* and stood patiently beside his wheelchair for several minutes and watched him, waiting for him to notice her.

He finally opened his eyes and saw her.

"Hel… hello," he said, surprised and more than a bit entranced.

"Hello. My name is Madhu. You are Joseph, yes?"

"Yes, I am," he smiled.

"Thank you for what you did for my brother Vijay yesterday. For coming to his aid and for playing with him. He gets lonely sometimes since our father died last year."

"Um, you're… you're welcome."

Madhu turned and began walking away.

"Wait," Joseph called out.

"Yes?" Madhu said as she turned back toward him.

"Where are you going?" he asked.

"I have to walk our cattle up the road so they may feed on the grass."

"Can I come with you?"

"Yes," she replied and smiled at him.

Minutes later, Madhu gently swung a long bamboo walking stick in the direction of the ten meandering cows, encouraging them to move along, as Joseph pushed himself in his wheelchair alongside her.

"You are from where, Joseph?"

"Montana. It's in America."

"I see," she replied.

Joseph nodded.

"Vijay tells me that you broke a piece of concrete with your fist," she said.

"Yeah, I learned it doing karate."

"What made you start karate?"

"It was just something to do," he lied.

"You have so much free time in America you have to look for things to do?"

"Oh, no. My dad kept us plenty busy," Joseph said, and then caught himself. "I'm sorry about that, about your dad and all."

"It is okay," Madhu replied.

"Don't you get any time for yourself?"

"When I am older there will be time," she said.

"Is everyone up here a farmer?"

"What else could they do, so far from the world? Men and boys work in the fields or raise cattle like we do. A woman works in the fields with her husband. Girls clean the house, do laundry, and wait to find a husband to start their own family. Since our father died, Vijay and I help my mother."

"What will happen when you get married? I mean, as far as work and stuff with your mother and Vijay. Will you still live with them?"

"Normally, I would move out into my husband's house to live with his family, but I will probably never know."

"Why is that?"

"Because up here a girl needs a dowry to give to her husband's family to get married."

"What's a dowry?"

"It is a gift from the bride's parents to the groom's parents at the time of marriage."

"I've never heard of such a thing," Joseph replied.

"I am told in the cities a girl has only to give her love to get married. We cannot afford to give up one of our cows because we need them to sell milk, so I may never get married."

"I see," Joseph said.

"Why did you come to India?" Madhu asked.

"To find Lahiri. Do you know him?"

The cows had made their way to delicious grass growing out of the side of the mountain, so Madhu sat down on a rock to let them graze. Joseph pushed his wheelchair up next to her.

"No one really knows him. I just know that he came down from the higher mountains when I was a little girl. There is a legend that he is three hundred years old. My great-grandmother once told me that her great-grandmother knew him as a boy. Others say he was never a boy and that he just appeared on Earth as an old man," she replied.

"Oh. So, I guess no one knows anything about his family?" Joseph inquired.

"I did not know he had a family. Where are they?"

"He said they died in an accident."

"Is that how you met?"

"No. We just kind of found each other and he is teaching me to walk again."

"How?" Madhu asked.

"With the power of mind over matter, but it's not going so well so far," he replied, looking down at his paralyzed limbs.

"I see. How did you become disabled?"

"I was on my way home from a karate tournament and a deer jumped out into the road and wouldn't move. It ran me into a tree and I broke my neck."

"Maybe it was someone dear," Madhu said.

"What's that supposed to mean?" Joseph asked.

"Maybe it was someone from a past life."

"Do you really believe in reincarnation?"

"There are hundreds of millions of people in India and most all of them believe in reincarnation."

"But why?"

"Because it is only logical. God is not cruel. He is trying to teach us what we need to learn, and giving us many opportunities to learn it," she said.

"But that doesn't make any sense. Every year there are more and more people in the world, so how could everyone be reincarnated?"

"Firstly, Joseph, there is too much to learn in just one lifetime. Secondly, do you really think this little planet is the only place life exists in the universe?"

"So some of us were former aliens?"

"I do not know exactly. I only know what I believe. What makes you believe Lahiri can teach you to walk again?"

"Because sages can do mind over matter, and when he teaches me I'll use it to walk with the power of my mind."

"Do you know what the name Lahiri means?"

"No," he answered.

"It means 'guardian.'"

Weeks later, Lahiri stood outside his front door as he yelled back inside and beckoned for Joseph to join him.

"Hurry, Joseph! You are going to make us late."

Joseph wheeled himself outside.

"What's the big hurry?" he asked.

Lahiri pointed to the sky, which was heavy and full of dark clouds.

"See those clouds?"

"How could I miss them?" Joseph replied.

"Monsoon season is upon us. We must get into town before the rains begin so that we may contribute and pay homage for nourishing our crops."

Two hours later and fifty yards from the outskirts of town, where the festival was in full swing, the skies opened up in a way that Joseph had never witnessed. Growing up in the Montana foothill mountains he was not unaccustomed to heavy rains, but still he had never seen anything like this before.

India's lush greenery and foliage could be traced back to the unique weather pattern of the monsoon rains. They started at the southern tip of the Indian subcontinent in late May and worked their way thousands of miles north to the Himalayan mountain range by September. For most of India the three or four months of often constant rain was all they would receive for the entire year, so it was critical for the crops and the people whose lives depended upon them.

The raindrops falling on Joseph were large enough to cause small animals to run for cover. Dozens of villagers were adorned in intricate ceremonial outfits with bright colors and floral design patterns, garland after garland of flowers, and handcrafted necklaces. Many had temporary tattoos on their hands and arms of henna – a vegetable dye. Others danced in elaborate routines as an expression of their appreciation for life itself.

Even those not dancing were jostled from side to side, soaked to the bone, and completely happy. Joseph searched the crowd for Madhu. He found her across the street dancing with several of her friends.

It took him a few attempts to make his way through the crowd over to her in his wheelchair.

"Will I see you tonight?" he asked.

Madhu smiled and nodded.

By midnight the rains had tired of their onslaught and were resting until the morning. The moon was barely one quarter full, but still provided ample light for Joseph and Madhu. She sat on a rock next to his wheelchair as she played on a small flute. Her melody was beautiful and soothing. She finished her musical poetry and placed the instrument down next to her on the rock.

"Providing entertainment to a husband's family is just one of the many important duties a wife must perform," she said and smiled at him.

"You're worth it just for the music," he said, smiling back.

"Tell me about your family, Joseph."

"My dad owns a bottling plant back in Montana. My brother Billy runs it with him."

"But you did not want to do that?"

"What makes you say that?" he asked, impressed by her intuitive nature.

"If you did you would not be here," she replied.

"Oh, right. No, I mean, the ranch is beautiful. Dad raises horses and stuff."

"Why are you not married?"

"Wow, you ask a lot of questions. But I like that. What will happen when you get married?" Joseph deflected.

"I will probably never know unless my mother will part with some of our cows. She had hoped I would only cost her one cow, but now it may be three and then she and Vijay would never survive," she said ruefully.

"Hmm," was all Joseph could say.

"Do you not miss your family?" she asked.

"Very much. But even before the accident that maimed me, I knew I'd have to leave someday. I just never thought it would be in a wheelchair."

"Montana sounds like a beautiful place."

"It is. I have a nephew back home I haven't seen since he was a few months old."

"Will you go back home soon?"

"I don't know. Sometimes this place feels like home."

"Maybe it was," Madhu offered.

"What do you mean?"

"Have you ever asked Lahiri why he came looking for you? Or why he took you into his home?"

"No. I just figured he likes to help people."

"So, then he traveled halfway around the world to offer you help at a karate match, and then he also just happened to be the man you came halfway back around the world to find?"

"I don't know. I just figured it was by chance."

"Nothing happens in life by chance."

"I guess," Joseph said.

"Maybe you were his son in a past life who died in that accident."

CHAPTER 10

Joseph's mother stood at her kitchen counter and lifted the sliced vegetables from the cutting board onto a serving plate. She had a good many guests in her living room waiting for more appetizers. Lily stood next to her and mixed homemade salad dressing as Billy wandered in. He hoped that he could appear interested in helping without actually having to do so – cooking was not his thing.

"Can I help?" he asked, straining to sound sincere but not confident that he had pulled it off.

He gave Lily a kiss on the cheek for good measure. She knew exactly what he was doing, but let him off the hook just the same.

"You can help by making sure James stays out of mischief," Lily said.

"Mischief? How much mischief can a three-year-old get into?" he countered, feeling the need to stand up for his young son, regardless of the trouble Billy knew he was more than likely getting into.

Mrs. Connell laughed and said, "Do you remember when Joey was..."

She stopped filling the bowel and trailed off without finishing her question, upset by her own memories.

Billy made his way closer to his mother and took the ladle from her hand.

"I'll do that, Mom," he said.

Mrs. Connell walked out of the kitchen and into the living room, where she walked under a banner that read, "Happy 25th Wedding Anniversary Bonnie & John," and feigned for some way to distract herself. Billy and Lily walked into the living room as well, each holding a bowl of food that they placed on the buffet table.

Billy quickly scanned for James, now that he had prematurely vouched for his good behavior. He found his little bundle of joy standing at a night table by the couch. On the table rested three pictures in frames. James picked up the one of Billy and Joseph, as Billy walked over to him and knelt beside his son. James pointed to his father in the picture.

"That's you, Daddy," he said.

"Yes, honey, that's Daddy," Billy replied.

James pointed to Joseph. "Who's that, Daddy?"

"That's your Uncle Joey."

"What's an uncle?"

Billy sighed and replied, "That means he's my brother and your second daddy."

"Oh, where is he?" James asked.

"He went away."

"Why?"

"To find himself," was all Billy could think to say.

"Did he get lost, Daddy?"

"Yes, honey, he did," Billy replied with a heavy heart.

"Why doesn't he just call?" James responded.

Billy scooped his little boy into his arms, stood up, and replied as much for his own comfort, "He will, James. He will."

Mr. Connell tapped a spoon against a glass while standing under the anniversary banner with his wife.

"If we could have everyone's attention, please?" he called out.

Everyone in the house stopped chatting and turned their attention toward Mr. and Mrs. Connell.

"First, to my beautiful wife, Bonnie, I want to say thank you for the priceless twenty-five years of happiness you have given me," Mr. Connell said.

Guests clapped in agreement as Mrs. Connell gave her husband a kiss.

"And here's hoping she'll give me at least another twenty-five years," he continued and he kissed her back.

Friends continued to clap as Mr. Connell raised his glass and said, "And to our son, Joey, may we see him back home soon."

Everyone nodded in heartfelt agreement and took a sip from their drinks. Billy made his way over to his mother and father while still carrying James and holding Lily's hand.

"Uh, I, uh, I mean, we, that is Lily and me, we have something to add," Billy said.

He playfully pointed to himself and said, "Number one," pointed to Lily and said, "Number two," pointed to

James and said, "Number three," then pointed to Lily's belly and said, "Number four."

It took a moment, but then everyone clapped loudly in approval.

Lily called out to the room, "Now as some of you may know, you can't actually find out the sex of the baby until the fifth month, but since this is the Connell family we're talking about here, we've already named him Thomas Joseph Connell."

The room was ecstatic at the news except for Mrs. Connell, who wiped tears from her eyes as she hugged Billy and Lily warmly, then walked out onto the wrap-around porch to be alone with her thoughts.

Madhu sat on her favorite boulder, the one shaped perfectly for sitting next to Joseph in his wheelchair. Moonlight provided the only illumination.

"What made you so sure you could learn to walk again?" she asked.

"I didn't know what else to do. Nothing made sense. I thought about killing myself at home, but I kept thinking about who in my family would find me and how much pain that would cause them. And I didn't have the right to do that, not after all they've done my whole life is love me."

"And when you got here?"

"Well, actually, I snuck a tiny gun into India in my wheelchair frame and I did put it to my head and pull the trigger. But fortunately, Lahiri had stolen the bullet.

It wasn't because I'm paralyzed. I was just so tired and wanted to rest."

"It wasn't because you felt trapped?" she asked, with a slip of the tongue.

Joseph picked up on her slip but chose not to press her on it.

"Trapped in my own life, maybe. When I was six years old I started having nightmares. Soon they turned to more visions that were really happening to me. At first, I just screamed in terror. I wondered if they were demons or something. When I told my mother she took me to a doctor. He put me on some drugs but the visions only got worse... a lot worse. It was like they were trying to punish me for trying to escape them. By the time I was nine years old I just pretended to take the pills and learned not to scream anymore. I would hold them under my tongue and spit them out later. Billy knew but never told our parents."

"And you never told anyone after that?"

"What would have been the point? My family tried to reach me. But it was like they couldn't get in and I couldn't get out. I never feel what I'm supposed to. I try, but I can't. And I want to so bad. But now it's too late," he lamented.

"I do not believe you cannot feel anything, Joseph."

"Usually the visions happened while I was sleeping, but not always. Sometimes they would take over my reality. I'd just be sitting there and suddenly I'd see them. I'd see someone break into our house and try to kill my family. I knew they weren't real but it still tormented me. That's why I took up karate."

"Do you think you will ever learn to walk again, really?" she asked.

"I don't know. It's not going so well and not looking like it. I mean, I've learned some things. Like, we're all just like leaves on that tree over there. But I don't know if that has anything to do with learning to walk."

"There are more important things than walking, you know." Madhu said.

"Like what?"

"Like kissing," she replied and smiled at him.

Joseph smiled brightly as he leaned forward in his wheelchair. She leaned forward as well, meeting him in the middle, but just before they kissed Joseph pulled away.

"Why would you want to kiss me?" He asked while looking down at his maimed body. "I mean, look at me."

Madhu looked at him lovingly.

"Joseph, how is it that with such beautiful eyes you are so unable to see the world? Your body is injured, that is true. But you are not your body. That is just a temporary thing, like a coat you put on to go out. It is a vehicle for your spirit to do its work. And you have a beautiful spirit," she said as she caressed his scar lined face. "Every scar on your body, every limb that does not work, only makes me love you more. Do you want to know why?"

Joseph nodded.

"Because you are here doing more spiritual work each day in your struggles than many people do in a lifetime. Now, may I kiss you?" she asked.

A happy tear rolled down Joseph's left cheek as he leaned in and kissed her with a grateful heart.

One month later Lahiri and Joseph were out spending the afternoon by the river. On the other side a funeral was taking place. Dozens of family members and mourners gathered as four men carried the dead man and placed him on a funeral pyre – a large pile of branches that was soon to be set on fire.

"What's going on?" Joseph asked.

"The dead man is being prepared for his death passage. Notice that he is being carried on two bamboo sticks held together by rope only."

Joseph nodded as he continued.

"He has been washed, wrapped in a white cloth, and decorated with flowers. Relatives have placed holy water from the Ganges into his mouth for purification and to help him on his journey."

Some of the deceased man's relatives said prayers while others performed ceremonial chants and his oldest son circled his body three times, then lit his father on fire to cremate him and set his spirit free.

Lahiri leaned closer to Joseph and said, "This is the most important part. You must remember to... I mean, the oldest son, or whoever is closest to the deceased person, must circle his body three times."

"Okay," Joseph said.

"Remember, Joseph, three times," Lahiri repeated emphatically.

"Right, three times. Got it."

Joseph watched as the oldest son prayed while his father's body burned in ritual.

"If the deceased is believed to have obtained *Moksha*, the cloth wrapping the body should be yellow instead of white," Lahiri said.

"What is *Moksha*?" Joseph asked.

"*Moksha* is the final stage of enlightenment, when enough has been learned that no future physical incarnations are necessary."

"Oh."

"Now, do not forget, Joseph. Yellow, not white," Lahiri reminded him.

"Got it. Yellow, not white."

Later that night Joseph sat in his wheelchair at the desk in his room, writing a letter to his mother. He was near the bottom of the page. He had been telling Mrs. Connell about how the people of India seemed to find something to celebrate nearly every single day of the year, which was probably why they had so many millions of gods to worship.

He told her about how the sweltering heat was matched only by the freezing cold in the winter, so high up in the Himalayan mountains. He told her how he hadn't made any progress in learning to walk through meditation, but that he was starting to think that maybe he didn't really come to India to learn to walk after all.

He told his mother in his letter that maybe he had really come to India to fall in love, which had happened with Madhu. That he was going to ask her to marry him and to come back home to Montana with him, and give up learning to walk again. Joseph told his mother that he loved her, that he was sorry he hadn't written in so long, or hadn't told her that before. He asked her to tell his dad and Billy that he loved them too and that he would tell them himself when he saw them again soon.

On a distant mountain range that Lahiri had trekked to in order to ensure his solitude he sat meditating. Unlike his usual silent meditation he chanted this time. His sounds started out calmly and softly enough but as he continued they became louder and more insistent.

The purple energy field that surrounded him pulsated, unstable in nature.

Lahiri argued, in his own way, that any decision such as this should be his and no one else's. He put forth, in spirit, that he was the one who had orchestrated the meeting between Joseph and Madhu and that what was to come was not right.

He had argued. But had lost. For he had overplayed his machinations to orchestrate Joseph meeting Madhu and falling in love. So his wings were clipped, forces more powerful than he stepped in to fill the breech, and what came next was beyond his control. Joseph had not come to India to fall in love and abandon his destiny and so he would be redirected. As needed.

Lahiri's purple energy field pulsed once more, then evaporated as if extinguished in power.

His sense of guilt was crushing. Three days later, early in the morning, he stood at the table in the main room of his house. Joseph wheeled himself out from his bedroom expecting to see a hearty breakfast, but quickly noticed that the table was lacking in food.

"Hey? Where's breakfast?" he asked.

"Just a moment, please, Joseph," Lahiri softly replied.

"What?"

"Please. Just... one... moment more."

Joseph did as he was asked but the ensuing silence was broken by a knock at the door. A depleted Lahiri opened the door and Joseph was shocked at who stood in the doorway.

"Billy? What are you doing here?" he asked.

CHAPTER 11

For the largest funeral procession in the memory of this small Montana town, eight pallbearers carried the oversized casket of John and Bonnie Connell to their final resting place in Bonnie's favorite meadow, the one she loved to take in from her kitchen window.

Following closely behind, Billy pushed Joseph in his wheelchair as Lily carried baby Thomas Joseph Connell, while she gently held James's little hand. Hundreds of mourners followed them into the meadow and to the gravesite. The pallbearers lowered the casket to the ground.

Billy's hands were completely bandaged with small blood stains seeping through at the knuckles.

Pastor David led everyone in a hymn. Lily cried. Billy was numb, Joseph barely under control. As the hymn finished Pastor David addressed the mourners.

"Our Father in Heaven, we meet this day to honor the lives of John and Bonnie Connell and to try to offer comfort to those loved ones who are left behind, and thank Thee for all the blessings we enjoy. In the name of Jesus Christ, Amen."

Larry, a close friend of the family, walked to the podium to speak.

"I have been a friend of John and Bonnie Connell since before they were married. Since we were kids. John never stormed any beaches nowhere or won any medals. I can't even remember the last time Bonnie ever traveled further than town. They never much cared about money, no matter how much they had, but they were the richest people I have ever known, for the love they gave so freely to everyone they knew. Their friends, their children, and their grandchildren."

Joseph looked away and fought to not break down. Larry's comments, while honorable to his departed friends, were cutting into him like daggers.

"I know they will never be very far from us," Larry continued, "because they live every moment with us in our hearts."

He bowed his head and stepped aside.

Pastor David again addressed the crowd, "To every thing there is a season and a time to every purpose under Heaven."

Billy's friend Cody leaned over to their friend Greg.

Cody whispered to him, "Coroner pronounced them dead at the scene. Took four hours for the Jaws-Of-Life to cut the car in half and get their bodies out. The drunk who hit them was singing so loud in the back of the police car, Billy went berserk, broke the window with his fists, pulled the guy out, and started beating him to death."

"I wondered about those bandages on his hands until I heard what happened," said Greg.

"Guy was so drunk he didn't even remember killing Billy's parents or Billy knocking all his teeth out. Took four cops to pull Billy off of him and he decked two of them before some more could wrestle him to the ground long enough for the paramedic to inject him with a sedative. D.A. wanted to press charges against him for assaulting the officers. Chief of Police was at Billy's baptism and his sons' baptisms. Said he'd knock the D.A.'s teeth out himself if he pressed charges."

Pastor David closed his Bible and nodded to Billy, who softly returned the nod and gently ushered his oldest son, James, forward. The confused little boy placed a flower on top of the casket holding his dead grandparents, then stepped back to his father. A moment later the casket was slowly lowered into the ground. Joseph could barely breathe.

And with that... his parents were gone forever.

Back in the Connell house mourners filled the living room. With his breathing still partly arrested, Joseph wheeled himself over to his brother and Lily.

"Billy, did Mom get my letter?" he asked.

Still shell-shocked, Billy simply replied, "What?"

"Did Mom get my letter?" he repeated emphatically.

"She didn't mention anything. Why?"

"Where's the mail?" Joseph implored.

"I put all the mail from last week in their bedroom."

Joseph turned himself around and headed into his parents' bedroom, oblivious to the guests he bumped into along the way. Billy turned in confusion to Lily.

"Go after him," she said.

In his parents' bedroom Joseph rifled through the pile of mail on their dresser. He found his letter... unopened. He picked it up, growing more upset with each passing moment as Billy entered the room.

"Joey?" he softly called, unaware of the newest avalanche of anguish enveloping his little brother.

Unable to speak while his jaw quivered and tears streamed down his face into the corners of his mouth, Joseph handed his letter to Billy, who opened it and scanned it top to bottom. He finally reached the part that was tearing his brother apart. He knelt down next to him.

"She knew, Joey. They both did," Billy whispered.

He lowered the armrest to Joseph's wheelchair, hugged his grief-stricken brother, and wondered why life tormented him so. Billy cradled Joseph's weary head and rocked him gently, each sob from his baby brother another knife in his already wounded heart. Billy wanted to cry, for himself, for his parents, for his brother, but that would have to wait until later.

He just held Joseph and whispered, while caressing the back of his head, "They knew, Joey. They knew."

7 YEARS LATER

CHAPTER 12

As co-owner of the family bottling plant and in his third year as Chief Financial Officer after attending college and earning a finance degree, Joseph insisted on working considerably longer hours than Billy had told him were necessary. The thing was, Billy had his loving wife and two sons to go home to and all Joseph had was the empty house he grew up in and his wheelchair.

On more than one occasion Billy also joked that going through all the trouble to dress in slacks, dress shirt, and tie was not necessary; after all, they owned the company. But Joseph would not hear of it.

This Friday afternoon some new reports needed analyzing, though the task could have waited until Monday or Tuesday. Joseph sat at his desk, on the phone, talking to an assistant in the company accounting department when Billy wandered into his office. He held up his index finger. Billy smiled and sat down on the corner of his desk.

"Yeah, I've got the reports in front of me," Joseph said to the person on the phone. "Now, I want you to go back and calculate the difference to projected net income under both scenarios. First under the accelerated depreciation schedule, then under a capitalized lease deal."

He waited for an answer and then replied, "I'll be here until nine tonight. Call me if you have anything by then... Okay, fine, call me first thing Monday."

Joseph hung up the phone and looked up at Billy, who chimed in quickly to steer the conversation away from business.

"You're going to be on time for Thomas Joseph's birthday party tomorrow, right?" he asked.

"Already got his present wrapped and ready to be broken," Joseph replied.

"Does it make a lot of noise? Because Lily just loves those, you know. She can't prove it but she swears you do it on purpose."

"It does and I do," Joseph replied. "But tell her not to worry. This one is mommy friendly."

"Those reports tell you anything valuable, Mr. Fancy Chief Financial Officer?"

Joseph nodded and said, "I think the new technology's worth the investment. Net income will probably take a hit the first three years, but it looks like with fixed costs under control, variable cost goes down by a penny per bottle, so by year four cash flow should skyrocket."

"Not bad for a guy who used to steal bottles and use them for target practice," Billy playfully jabbed.

"Schooled you, didn't I?" Joseph protested.

"So when do you fly to Utah?"

"Tuesday. I've got a meeting with the Lieutenant Governor and State Treasurer. If I can get them to pony up another five million in tax breaks, we build our new plant there, if not, we'll just build it here in Montana," Joseph said.

Billy nodded, but had now had more than his fill of shop talk for a Friday afternoon.

"How did your date go last night?" he asked.

"I… uh… didn't go," Joseph admitted.

"Joey, why not? Jen's a great girl. She claims you sat next to her in the fifth grade and made faces at her all the time."

"Ah, I don't know. I mean, I've gotten used to being three feet tall and all, but…" Joseph trailed off.

"Do you know she's the third girl to ask Lily about you? What'd you do, find their sweet spot in high school or something?"

Joseph laughed.

"No, I did not, that's for sure. But who has time anyway?" he said.

"Don't you want to fall in love again? Whatever happened to Madhu? Why didn't you bring her back home to Montana?"

Joseph was lost in thought for a moment.

"I wrote to her for years. Maybe she didn't want to leave her family? Maybe she didn't want to marry a… I don't know. I sent her money for a dowry so her mother wouldn't have to sell any of the family cows."

"What's a dowry?" Billy asked.

"Doesn't matter," Joseph replied.

"Right. Listen, you want to come over for dinner tonight? Lily's making her world famous pot roast. The way you like it where the beef falls apart when you stick your fork in it."

"No, thanks. I've, uh, got to look over these reports again," Joseph lied.

"Okay. See you tomorrow then," Billy said as he stood up from the corner of the desk.

Joseph pretended to look over the reports, but only long enough until Billy turned the corner outside his office and walked down the hallway. Then he put down his pen and looked off into space, wondering about Madhu and what might have been.

The next day Joseph was on time for his nephew's seventh birthday party, as promised. He sat on the couch in Billy's living room next to Lily's friend, Jen. Thomas Joseph was surrounded by a dozen friends in preparation for blowing out the birthday candles on his ice cream cake.

Billy stood next to him.

"Do you know what you're going to wish for?" Billy asked his son.

Thomas Joseph nodded.

"What is it?"

Older brother James piped up, "Don't tell! If you do it won't come true."

Billy jumped in for damage control, "James, this is a special cake, it, um," he looked to Lily to bail him out, but she had nothing, so he stumbled forward on his own.

"It has chocolate ice cream… and… and the ice cream protects the wish, so it's okay," Billy said.

"That's ridiculous!" James declared.

Billy gave James a knock it off stare, which James did.

"Go ahead, T.J.," Billy continued with his more innocent son.

"I want a Mission Soldier," Thomas Joseph replied.

Billy looked over to his wife and said, "He wants a Mission Soldier, I wonder if he'll get it?"

Lily nodded.

"All right, T.J., if you blow out the candles read hard I bet your wish will come true," Billy said.

Thomas Joseph blew out the candles with determination. Billy picked his son up over his head and flew him around like an airplane.

Joseph leaned toward Jen and whispered, "I think James is about ready for some uncle interference, or I foresee a great many beautiful afternoons cleaning up more horse manure than one young boy is capable of shoveling. Maybe I'll just start slipping him a few hidden facts about his dear old dad."

"Save them," Jen replied. "You can start your uncle duties in a more important area. James has um, his first 'official' girlfriend."

Joseph chuckled.

"He's a bit young to embark on that torture. What chance has a boy got? The girl has all the cards."

Jen corrected him, "No, the boy has all the cards. The girl just has all the chips."

"Either way, it's a rigged game," Joseph protested.

Hours later Joseph sat in his wheelchair back on his family's ranch, just outside the corral nearest the barn. In his hand he held a pile of carrot pieces that he was feeding to Happy, who would have come over to keep him company even without the sweet orange treats in his hand. The sun had just begun to set over the nearest hilltop covered in an endless vista of Ponderosa pine trees.

"You, I should have taken over those hills more often when I had the chance," Joseph said.

While Happy ate from his hand Joseph looked into the barn and stared for a moment at his saddle still hanging on the wall that his father and brother had given him and below it the custom boots his mother had commissioned for him. The saddle had still never been ridden, the boots never been worn.

Billy quietly walked up from behind and watched him.

"Dad and I spent weeks figuring out what saddle to buy you, but Mom must have spent months making sure the bootmaker got every single detail correct from your sketches," Billy said and smiled.

"Yeah, they are both wonderful works of art. You could use the saddle if you want," Joseph offered.

"Oh, no, little brother. It's all yours," Billy replied affectionately.

"Remember when we were little and thought this ranch was so big it must cover the whole world?"

"Yeah, I do."

Joseph smiled but Billy could see that he was masking great sadness.

"Do you ever miss India, Joey?"

"Yeah, sometimes. I mean, I miss Madhu and maybe, I don't know, maybe I didn't finish what I started."

"You never really talk about your time over there."

Joseph sighed, "Well, when I got there I thought I'd just figure out that mind over matter trick and be able to walk again, no problem. But it wasn't that simple. Lahiri tried to teach me that there's more to it than that, because you have to learn something else first."

"Did you ever learn what it was?" Billy asked, intrigued.

"Yeah. But I didn't realize it until I got back home. I learned that one person hurting another really is like a hand curling into a fist to smash the foot. And that all that really matters is family and the people we're supposed to love, the people we know and even the people we don't. And that the purpose of life is to find the Light of God, but not the light from some old guy with a white beard sitting up there judging us. The light is the love we give each other on our way back home."

Billy was stunned at the words of wisdom coming from his little brother.

"Who taught you all that?" he asked.

"Well, Lahiri started it, but I didn't really put it all together until I got back home here, so you did… and Mom and Dad. For sure, Mom and Dad," Joseph said softly.

"My God, Joey, you learned more in three years over there than you did in your whole life back here."

"Yeah, I suppose it wasn't a total waste of time," Joseph replied.

"I'm sorry, Joey."

"Sorry? What for?"

"For being selfish. I love you so much that I've been keeping you here."

"You haven't been keeping me here, Billy."

"Yes, I have. And it's not right."

"I don't understand," Joseph replied.

"You don't belong here, Joey. You belong back in India to finish what you started."

"No… Billy. That was just a pipe dream a naïve kid had a long time ago. But that kid's dead now," Joseph wistfully replied.

"The hell he is."

Billy's softness was gone, for he had made up his mind.

"You don't belong here anymore, little brother, and I won't let you stay," he said firmly.

CHAPTER 13

Joseph arrived by oxen cart to the front of Lahiri's house, but his heart sank. The farmer unloaded his wheelchair and helped him into it, then turned and departed. The house had clearly been abandoned for years. He wheeled himself inside but the dust strewn interior only confirmed what he already knew.

He spent hours straightening up and sweeping out what he could. Then made his way to Madhu's house, with no idea if she would even still be there. He knocked on the front door of her house with a lump in his throat, but it melted away when it was Madhu who answered the door.

"Joseph, come in," she beamed with affection.

They sat at the small table inside her house.

"I wasn't sure you'd still be here," he said.

"Where else would I be?" she replied.

"Thought maybe you'd be married. Thought you'd use the money for a dowry."

Madhu stood up and walked to a small dresser drawer, reached in and retrieved an envelope full of cash in U.S. dollars, then sat back down at the table with it.

"How could I be married? The man I am supposed to marry left."

Joseph choked up.

"I'm sorry."

"Do not be sorry, Joseph. You did what you had to do."

"He's gone."

"Lahiri?" Madhu asked.

Joseph nodded, "Probably back up in the higher mountains."

"Then go find him."

Joseph looked down at his maimed body, "I can't."

Madhu reached out with love that had never waived and touched him on the arm, "Then I will find him."

She searched days and nights for Lahiri in even more remote villages higher up in the mountains. Through wilderness he might have retreated to so that he could be truly alone. But on the fifth day she walked back through the door to Lahiri's house. Joseph looked up and there he saw Lahiri enter behind her.

And so Joseph's work was renewed. Lahiri took him to the highest mountain peak his wheelchair could navigate, high up among the clouds. Joseph meditated with deep breaths, a still mind, and an open heart.

"Breathe, Joseph. Breathe deeply and purely and you will come to know all that you are meant to see," Lahiri said supportively.

With sturdy determination Joseph continued his meditation.

"You will first begin to feel the seven *chakras* along your spine awaken and grow in size and energy and power.

They may feel no larger than a tiny pebble but I will help you to sense them and as they awaken and their energy grows, your insights will grow along with them. You will see that you are not a spirit trapped in a body. For your body is more than a container of flesh. It is a vessel to reconnect your spirit to the infinite," Lahiri guided him.

"As your mind expands in awareness you will channel the energy of the universe," he continued.

Joseph sat still in meditation, as ancient seers had for done thousands of years before, and he found that he could see beyond the apparent limited reality that his five senses offered to him. He could feel that his body was only solid matter when viewed from without, but when viewed from within, it was layer upon layer of energy vibrations.

He could feel his *chakras* awakening all up and down his spine.

"Everywhere, Joseph, are dimensions unseen until you are ready to receive them. The past. The departed. The invisible. They are all around you. They are all open and available to you," Lahiri taught him.

"I can see now," said Joseph. "The night of my accident I tried to leave my body, but you wouldn't let me."

"I could not. For then you would not have lived out what we were meant to live. Together."

Joseph relived all of his visions that tormented him. But now he saw that in each one of them Lahiri was there in spirit, watching over him.

Joseph's vision of the four lions resumed. He saw himself pinned on the ground by the leader of the lion pack. He looked at the terrifying beast above his face, but for the first time he did not feel any fear. In that instant the lion fell dead, as did the other three with it.

He stood up and looked down at the four dead lions, the three dead warriors, and the dead deer that had maimed him.

They all rose from the ground and morphed into their true being – *Spirits Of White Light.* For they were not demons but spirits summoned for duty, as Joseph was about to learn.

They flew toward a bright glowing light ahead of them. He followed.

He walked through the glowing light and found himself back in time, here at the same stone white house. But in the past he was a British soldier in his forties. Dozens of other soldiers in 19th century uniforms stood at attention, for he was their Commanding Officer. All of the soldiers carried single shot rifles. Joseph could see that the sword that hung from his military uniform was the *same sword* he carried when he fought the warriors in his visions.

Standing in front of Joseph-The-Soldier were two lower-ranking men who each held tightly the arm of an Indian man who was their prisoner.

Not far from Joseph-The-Soldier was Billy, also dressed in the same uniform, but of a lower rank than Joseph-The-Soldier.

Joseph could see that the Indian man being held *was a younger Lahiri*, only aged twenty-five. And off to his right were soldiers who also held as prisoners Lahiri's wife and two young boys, ages five and two. His wife held their youngest son in her arms. The boys cried, his wife stood with a terrified look on her face.

The soldier on Lahiri's left spoke up.

"Caught him trying to incite a mutiny, Sir."

"Are you certain he was trying to incite an insurrection?" Joseph-The-Soldier asked.

"He does not deny it, Sir," the soldier replied.

Joseph-The-Soldier reflected for a moment and then came to a decision.

"It burdens me to say this, but... it must be done. Put him and his family to death," he ordered.

Billy-The-Soldier was aghast at what he had just heard.

"Joseph... I mean, Commander Connell, may I have a word, please?" Billy-The-Soldier requested.

Joseph-The-Soldier nodded and they walked several feet away to speak in private.

"Please, Joseph, I beg of you. Not as your junior officer, but as your dearest friend, do not do this thing you have ordered."

"It gives me no pleasure, William. I do what I must to keep civilized peace in this region. You know as well as I what happened two years ago in the Mutiny of 1857. Thousands on both sides were tortured and killed, Indians and British subjects alike. If I do as you wish and a new mutiny spreads and thousands more die in this province that it is my sworn duty to govern, women and children included, will their blood be on my hands or yours?"

Billy-The-Soldier was not so easily swayed from his sense of higher moral responsibility.

"Joseph, you have ordered the murder of innocent civilians, of a mother and her two small boys, in addition to the man who is their father. We have lived more of our lives stationed here in India than in our native England. To have these people killed here now is no less heinous an act of murder than if they had been our neighbors back in Carlisle when we were just boys," he implored.

"My friend, I mean these people no ill will. My order is not born out of malice or disaffection for their lives, this fate they must now meet. It is unfortunate that they must perish."

"But they are not to perish, Joseph," Billy-The-Solder argued. "They are to be murdered, by *your* order. When we were boys it was you to fought for the underdog, who gave the bully the beat down."

Billy-The-Soldier pointed over to Lahiri's wailing wife and crying sons.

"These people are the underdog. But instead of fighting for them, you murder them. Kill their father if you must, I concede. But please do not murder his family."

"It is my duty, William."

"Murder is never one's duty."

Joseph-The-Soldier was flummoxed. Had this been anyone but his best friend from boyhood, not only would the order have already been carried out but Billy would have been brought up on charges of insubordination.

However, this was not any other soldier.

Joseph-The-Soldier walked over to Lahiri, who looked back at him with eyes full of hatred. The soldiers nearby, upon hearing Joseph's order of death, had raised their rifles and pointed them at Lahiri to ensure that no danger came to them or their commanding officer who had just made his decision.

Joseph-The-Soldier motioned for Billy-The-Soldier to join him.

He then turned to face Lahiri.

"Sir," he said to him. "I ask you, upon your word as a gentleman, if you had not been discovered by my sentry, did you mean to bring mortal harm upon me, my men, and even upon my friend here who now pleads for the lives of your family?"

"Yes, I most certainly did," a defiant Lahiri icily responded.

"Why?" asked Joseph-The-Soldier.

"Because you invade our country as if it is your Divine right to do so. You command us how to live, take what of our possessions you desire as taxes, and instruct us to be happy with what you choose to leave for us. If I invaded your country, plundered your riches, taxed your possessions, and ordered you to be happy with my rule and dominion over you and your family, would you not do as I have attempted to do, even if it meant the death of me and my countrymen?" Lahiri replied.

"So I would, Sir. So I would," Joseph-The-Soldier responded respectfully.

Any final hope that Billy-The-Soldier harbored of sparing lives today was dashed by the next exchange.

"And, Sir," Joseph-The-Soldier continued. "Even if I were to release you and your family today, would you not come back again and try to murder us all?"

"I most certainly would," a still defiant Lahiri replied.

Joseph-The-Soldier reached into his breast pocket with his left hand and pulled out a coin, with the date printed on it of 1859. It was the *same coin* that Joseph had found in the book he was reading in the white stone house that belonged to Lahiri in the present day after it had belonged to him in his past life.

He handed the coin to Lahiri.

"I respect you, Sir. For your honesty and integrity, though they may conflict with the directives of my army and even with the continuation of my life. You may use this coin to buy one last meal for your family and say a proper goodbye, compliments of Her Majesty and the Crown of England, Ruler of India."

The two soldiers holding Lahiri escorted him away, still with rifles pointed at him by their fellow soldiers. As all the men walked farther away, Joseph-The-Soldier was left alone with Billy-The-Soldier, who stared at him in disbelief.

"You've got to decide if your actions are worth the cost. It is that simple," Joseph-The-Soldier said.

Billy-The-Soldier sadly shook his head.

"I do as my conscience guides me, William."

"I fear for the fate of your soul, Joseph."

"My angels will protect me."

"And if your angels should attack you for what you bring to bear this day?"

Joseph-The-Soldier moved his left hand and placed it symbolically over his sword that hung from his sash.

"Then I welcome their deeds at the place of my reckoning. If there be consequences not of my desire in this life or in the unknown hereafter, then I accept them willingly. And if feral beasts should torment me for what I do here today, then may they at least do so where I can ride my majestic horses through the hills and enjoy the beauty of this world, wherever that beauty may be," Joseph-The-Soldier replied.

"I will pray for you, Joseph, as I will pray for all of us here today. You are not only my dearest friend but you have saved my life more than once and for that, I will accompany you wherever your deeds and travels may take you," Billy-The-Soldier said with a heavy heart, then walked silently away.

Later that night Joseph-The-Soldier sat at the desk in his bedroom, the same room that Lahiri had given him to use in this lifetime. He was in the midst of writing a letter on parchment paper to his superiors about the events that had taken place earlier in the day. He paused for a moment in reflective thought, then continued writing.

He expressed his sentiment that while the events were unfortunate, in his honest estimation they were unavoidable in the larger picture of keeping the peace by setting the example that insurrectionists would be granted no quarter for themselves nor their families.

Joseph-The-Soldier was about to sign his letter when a hand reached around from behind him and dragged him to the floor.

It was an enraged Lahiri with madness in his inflamed eyes. He bludgeoned Joseph-The-Soldier over the head repeatedly with a wooden club, drawing significant blood but not knocking him unconscious.

"You had my family killed! You should have had them kill me first, then I could not have escaped and now give you what you deserve," Lahiri intoned in a low voice so nearby soldiers could not hear him.

He bashed Joseph in the head one final time, purely to inflict more pain before meting out his own form of final justice.

"My sons were only five and two years old. They and my beautiful wife did not deserve to have their throats slashed. As you have no family here for me to kill, I will send you alone to my babies and wife so that you may explain to them yourself why you had them murdered!" Lahiri cried.

As blood flowed profusely from the head of Joseph-The-Soldier, Lahiri pulled out a twelve-inch dagger, the *same dagger* that Joseph had found early in his arrival back in India, and thrust it with all his might into his mortal enemy at the solar plexus, at the top of the abdomen. In the exact same spot that Joseph in this lifetime was born with the pink, jagged-shaped scar at the top of his abdomen.

The birthmark that had so interested Lahiri the night he approached Joseph in the locker room after his ribs had been shattered in the karate tournament.

Once the dagger was firmly in the flesh of Joseph-The-Soldier, Lahiri twisted it forcefully, making sure there was no question that the wound would be fatal.

He then fled the scene of the murder still holding the bloody dagger.

As Joseph still sat in his wheelchair meditating with Lahiri by his side, his vision picked up the day after his own murder.

Outside the white stone house, Billy-The-Soldier sat atop his horse. A low-ranking soldier stood in front of him and made a report.

"Lieutenant, Sir, we have combed this village and the surrounding areas for days. The murderer Lahiri is nowhere to be found," reported the man.

"And you are sure he is not hiding in any villages nearby?" Billy-The-Soldier asked.

"We are sure, Sir," the soldier replied, then pointed off into the higher Himalayan mountain ranges. "He is somewhere deeper up there."

"I see," Billy-The-Soldier said sadly.

"Sir, how long do you think he can survive up there?" the soldier asked.

"A hundred years, maybe longer for all I know. However long he does survive he will no doubt have a great many things weighing on his soul."

"Yes, Sir."

"Have the men assemble," Billy-The-Soldier ordered and gave the soldier a salute.

The soldier returned the salute, then turned and walked off in the distance to go assemble the men.

Billy-The-Soldier sighed and looked up into the nearby mountains, then up into the heavens above.

"God speed to you, Joseph. May we see each other again soon enough," he whispered.

The vision faded as Joseph trembled in his wheelchair, reliving all the pain that he had set in motion so very many years ago.

The spirits of Joseph's parents appeared before him. He began to cry.

"I'm sorry, Mom and Dad. For causing your deaths, for getting off track here in India," he said.

Joseph's mother spoke with pure love for her and Mr. Connell, "My dear sweet boy, do not be sorry. We agreed to be your parents before you were born. Before even we were born. Come what may. You did not rob us of our destiny. You helped us complete it."

Joseph smiled through his tears as the spirits of his parents disappeared.

The Wheels Of Light along his spinal column grew in size until they merged into a ball of light and from the light Joseph could see the fugitive Lahiri running for his life. He outran the soldiers who pursued him and slowed to a walk, then exhausted he sat down.

And from that seated position he began his meditation. Over many years and decades in the safety of isolation he continued to meditate. His hair and beard grew long, then gray, then fell out through the passage of time.

Joseph could see that Lahiri was trapped, his penance was that he was not permitted to die, but required to remain alive until Joseph was reborn so that they could heal what had taken place between them. And so when Joseph was reborn as the younger brother to the Connell family, Lahiri arose from his decades upon decades of meditation and returned to the long ago abandoned stone white house that they were soon meant to share.

And as Joseph grew into a young boy Lahiri secretly visited him again and again in Montana, always keeping a safe distance. Always waiting, until the time was right to approach him. Until Joseph had been permitted to live out his years as a boy. Until the clock struck the time of his birth when he became a man on his eighteenth birthday and their date with destiny was upon them.

Lahiri stood in the center of the stone white house that had once belonged to Joseph-The-Soldier alone, then to Lahiri alone, and finally to Lahiri and Joseph together. He smiled with warmth and love as a hand gently extended toward him.

He clasped the hand of Joseph with tenderness and forgiveness was gladly given by both.

The wheel of karma that had been crushing them both beneath its suffocating weight had finally been lifted.

CHAPTER 14

In a small Montana airport waiting at the arrival gate a five-year-old boy jumped into his grandfather's arms.

"What are we doing here, Grandpa?" the boy asked.

The grandfather was Billy, aged seventy-two years old. He was about to answer his young grandson when Lily gently touched him on the arm, causing him to look up. Over to the doorway that led into the airport from the plane.

And there Billy saw his seventy-year-old little brother slowly walking toward him. Wearing for the first time the boots his mother had made for him on his tragic eighteenth birthday so very many years ago.

Joseph walked hand in hand with his loving wife, Madhu.

He made his way toward the older brother he loved with all his heart, whom he had not seen in forty-two years. For that was how long it took him to sit and breathe and summon the supernatural abilities to channel the energies of the universe that bridged his body and spirit.

In this moment walking in body and gratitude Joseph thought back about Lahiri, whom he had respectfully cremated on a funeral pyre before leaving India for the last time.

Joseph had wrapped him in the yellow cloth as requested, for they both agreed that the old man had not only obtained *Moksha*, but most certainly earned it as well, and was now free to continue his spiritual journey without the need for further physical reincarnations.

And as Joseph lit his dear friend on his death fire, he placed next to Lahiri the dagger that his friend had used to murder him in revenge. An emotion long since extinguished by both.

But before even Joseph had seen his dear friend off he walked with Lahiri through the maze of rocks in the backyard that had kept him from the tombstones. He had knelt before Lahiri's wife and two young sons and asked for their forgiveness.

Lahiri had smiled and let him know that his wife and two boys had already long ago forgiven Joseph as they had forgiven him for deciding that his cause was more important than their lives.

And here now, tears of joy welled up in the eyes of both elderly brothers as emotion washed over them. They wrapped their arms around each other with all the strength that would be summoned and a gentle smile came across Joseph's aged face.

His hair had long since turned gray and his scarred face was full of lines from a lifetime spent in the penetrating Indian sun.

But in his eyes was the peace it had taken him so very long to earn.

Joseph rested his head on Billy's shoulder.

He was finally home, with God in his heart.

THE END

Made in the USA
Middletown, DE
24 May 2021